Traded
Paperback Copyright © 2022 Lorhainne Ekelund
Editor: Talia Leduc

ISBN-13: 978-1998775088

Give feedback on the book at:
lorhainneeckhart@hotmail.com

Twitter: @LEckhart
Facebook: AuthorLorhainneEckhart

Printed in the U.S.A

Traded

THE WILDE BROTHERS

LORHAINNE ECKHART

Jake Wilde has two loves, but neither is going his way.

The Wilde Brothers

Come and meet the Wilde Brothers of Idaho. Joe, Logan, Ben, Samuel, and Jake. You'll love the western flair and hot men and strong women in this romantic family saga.

The One
The Honeymoon
Friendly Fire
A Matter of Trust
The Reckoning
Traded
Unforgiven
The Holiday Bride

Jake Wilde, the youngest of the Wilde brothers, has it all. He's a pro football star with the woman of his dreams by his side…or so he thought.

In a desperate attempt to keep the woman he loves, he asks her to marry him. The last thing Jake Wilde expects is for her to turn him down and walk out the door at the same time that his football team decides to trade him.

Chris Jeger, a legal assistant and part-time cheerleader for the Cardinals, has been waiting for true love. When she overhears Jake Wilde making a personal plea to some woman on the phone, she can see he's heading down the road to disaster. Instead of walking away, she steps in to offer him advice so he doesn't turn his life upside down the same way she once did.

Their friendship develops, and one night their emotions collide—but when someone unexpected suddenly knocks on his door, Jake learns that sometimes, what you wish for isn't what you really want. As real life interferes with her hopes and dreams, will Chris once again be brokenhearted, left on the outside looking in?

CHAPTER
One

"Son, that's the way things work here. You being traded is a part of life, and Phoenix is a great team, a great place to live. It's hot, never rains, and has plenty of women to choose from."

Jake stared into the deep-set blue eyes of Murray Donnelly, his about-to-be former coach for the Seahawks. The man had a heavily lined face and thin white hair, and he rapped his knuckles on the desk before leaning back in his chair. He had been behind this crappy old beat-up desk in the basement office for probably half a century. Hell, the team could afford better, *had* better, but Murray had a thing for old and beat up. Or so Jake often thought.

He squirmed in the wooden chair, and it squeaked under his weight. It wasn't that he was overweight: Jake Wilde, the youngest of the Wilde brothers, was in the best shape, he figured, of his football career. At six foot two and packing a solid 230 pounds, all lean and hard muscle, he wondered if the chair would hold his weight.

It sometimes seemed like all the furniture around him had been made for a kid.

"Look, I know you didn't want this, but let's get real, son. You're young, in the prime of your life, and you've already been out with how many injuries?" Murray scowled and then ran his tongue over his coffee-stained teeth. He wasn't much to look at, but he'd kicked Jake's ass from one end of the field to the other and had been the closest thing to a father that he'd ever had—that is, next to Logan, his older brother.

It hurt to be tossed away, turned away by a man he'd thought would fight for him.

"Cardinals are a good team. Bucky Phillips is a good coach."

Jake wasn't a moron. Murray always called out in great detail who was who and who sucked big time. Jake wondered if he'd had to choke out the "good" part, as Murray and Bucky were about as friendly as two hounds circling the same bitch. His lips actually twitched when he pictured them both snarling in the same undignified way.

"Look, son." Murray fidgeted in his chair, leaning back, resting his elbow on the seat arm as he turned to the side. He pulled away just enough that Jake could tell the old man was getting nervous. Feelings were the one thing this man didn't do, didn't talk about.

"I know, Coach. It wasn't your decision." At least he hoped it wasn't. He spied a flash of color on Murray's cheeks. Maybe he was wrong. His stomach tightened at the thought that Coach could be responsible for sending him on his way.

He cleared his throat, which thickened when he thought too much. Reading too much into a situation was one of his flaws. "So I'm replacing Brown?" he said. "He was a second-round pick, a favorite." He couldn't say anything else, as he knew he had tough shoes to fill. Brown had been fast, but Jake was faster—or had been before his ACL tear. Now the Phoenix quarterback would be looking for Jake on that field, and it was their relationship, the trust between them, that would mean the difference between winning and losing and being part of that team.

"Yeah, Brown's out. Tough card he got dealt with that last injury. Retired young, retired early. But not you." Coach swung around, setting his feet on the ground and standing up, sticking his hand out to Jake. It was his way of saying they were done, so long, get out of here.

It was awkward and impersonal. Jake thought the old man would have hugged him after all they'd been through: the games, hotels, traveling, training. They had been closer than family at one time, or so he thought. He stood up, feeling a twinge in his knee, and shook the old man's hand, looking down at him.

Murray slapped his shoulder with his other hand. "Get out of here, and make sure you listen to the doc. Stick with your physio. You can't afford any more injuries, because right now the entire world is watching you."

Jake knew what he was saying. The football world was the only world that existed for the coach. Anyone or anything else out there was a nobody.

CHAPTER

Two

As soon as his thumb pressed the numbers on his cell phone, he knew he shouldn't have made the call. *Hang up now, stupid!* his head screamed at his heart. This was one of those idiotic things Jake couldn't stop himself from doing. He felt, at times, as if he were part of a train wreck.

He walked along the end zone as the phone rang, watching his team—his former team—practice. He loved the grunts, the whistles, the plays called, the sweat, the running, everything about the game. And he'd loved this team.

Two rings and no answer. Dammit, he didn't want to leave another message, because he knew he was starting to sound pathetic. Three rings…

"Hey, Jake, wait up!" Glen Chalmer, the team physician who'd benched him, was jogging his way. Lean, middle aged, average, he was a man who wouldn't stick out in any crowd—but he was also a dick, considering he overlooked injuries all the time, all except Jake's. For some reason, Glen had it in for him. It had to be that.

Four rings. "Hi, this is Jill. I can't take your call. Leave a message and I'll call you back."

Shit! He held up his hand and gave Glen his back. "Hey, Jill, this is Jake…" Crap, did his voice sound weak and pathetic? Of course she knew it was him. She was probably screening this call just like all the others he had made. "I know I said I'd give you some space, but I wanted to let you know I'm leaving tonight—for Arizona…Phoenix," he said for emphasis, as if she didn't have a clue where he was going or had missed all the other messages he'd left.

He took the phone and smacked it against his forehead a couple times, then noticed the doc frowning. Maybe Glen had picked up on how desperate he was sounding. "I hoped you'd call me back before now. It's been…how long?" Twenty-six days and counting, and it was almost the end of the season. "I'd still love for you to come with me. So…call me." He made himself hit the "End call" button and pocket his cell phone as he jammed his fingers through his thick, dark hair. He could feel the ends, longer than they should be, but he'd let it grow, stopped shaving. Stopped caring, really.

"Glen," he bit out. He knew he sounded like a prick, but he didn't care. Glen was the last person to whom he wanted to extend any bit of civility. He crossed his arms over his wide chest, his navy hoodie pulling against his back. He took a breath, puffing out his chest, letting Glen sweat just a bit at the sight of the pissed-off hulk of a guy staring back at him. Jake was big enough, strong enough, built enough that he could make a man nervous when he wanted. And right now, he just didn't give a shit about playing nice.

"Just wanted to see how you're doing, how that last

checkup went for you with the ortho specialist I sent you to," Glen said.

See how he was doing, his ass. Jake started to say something, then glanced up and away for a second. "Fine," he said. "Take care, Glen. Got to go."

He started to turn away when the man reached out and touched his arm. Seriously. Jake's gaze went right there, to that light, slender hand on his bulging right bicep. He just stared at it with loathing, as if Glen had any hope in hell of holding him back.

Instead of using his words, as he knew Logan, his big brother, would have warned him—damn him, too, for being in his head—he reached down, lifted Glen's hand from his arm, and took a step back.

Glen must have known that Jake wasn't in a mood to be messed with, as he raised his hands in surrender. "Sorry, I can see you're still a little upset. I'm sorry, Jake, but this is the business, and as the team physician, it's up to me to make sure you're okay. We're a team here. Everyone gets injured, some worse than others. It just happened that your injuries were back to back. You pushed yourself too hard, didn't let up. Listen, if you continue to push yourself, that knee injury won't heal. Stick with your physio."

The way he rattled it off, Jake wasn't interested. In fact, he started away again, one step, two steps across the turf.

"Jake," Glen called out.

He glanced over his shoulder at the team physician, who was wearing the same light khaki pants he always wore, the dark blue and white team jacket, the light green lettering with the Seahawks logo on the front. He wore it like he owned it as his hands rested on his hips.

"Your first stop tomorrow morning is at nine a.m. with the Cardinals' physician. He's expecting you. Don't be late."

Jake hesitated a second, giving his head a shake, then walked out of the stadium, feeling Glen's eyes burning into him the entire time. He was very aware of his phone in his pocket and willed it to ring, ignoring that sinking feeling of losing his home, his team, and, worse than anything, the girl he loved. His bags were packed, and he thought of the airline ticket he had bought for Jill, knowing deep down that if he could just talk to her one more time, he really believed he could convince her that moving to Phoenix would be the best thing for both of them.

CHAPTER
Three

He hated red. The color unsettled him. It was one of those things he hadn't given much thought to until it was shoved right in his face, firing him up much like a red blanket did a feisty bull. Everywhere he looked, there it was, that deep blood-red color. Red jerseys, red shorts, the banners, the seats…even the cheerleaders' pompoms were red. Added to that was the Arizona heat, a dry climate far different from the one he was used to. He never thought he'd say it in a million years, but he missed the rain, the clouds, the green, the ocean. He was homesick for Seattle even though he'd grown up in rural Idaho, with deep snow and long, cold winters, mountains all around them. Seattle had been his home, the first one of his adult life, since getting drafted as a first-round pick for the Seahawks. He'd been the favorite then, but oh, how things changed.

His gym bag tossed over his shoulder, Jake watched the team, the Cardinals, training on the field from the sidelines. He chewed a piece of gum as he took in the players running and tackling, then the whistle blowing and the coaching staff yelling. He spotted Jeger, a wide receiver, running a pass. The man was fast and had been with the team a long time, but the play he had called out at the line last year, when he'd fumbled the ball and cost them the season, would forever be his legacy. It was the type of screwup every player prayed would never happen.

"So you made it." Bucky Phillips rested a hand on his shoulder. Jake had forgotten how tall the man was, this man he had never understood. He was in good shape and stood eye to eye with Jake, and he wore dark glasses and his trademark Cardinals cap, his sandy hair sticking out at the sides. He wore blue jeans, his arms tanned in his white golf shirt. His smile revealed white teeth, but Jake knew all too well that with men like Bucky, a smile only hid what they were really thinking.

"Arrived last night." It had been after nine when he checked in to the Westin, alone, his home away from home until he found a new place to live, and as the hours ticked by and he'd been forced to board the plane alone, he had felt the distance from the girl he loved, who wouldn't return his calls.

"Great to hear, great to hear. Heard you checked in with Danny." The man didn't say anything else, only pulling his hand away and letting it fall to his side. Jake wondered, when the coach said nothing else, whether the doctor had told him something he should be worried about.

"Yeah, I'm anxious to get out there."

The smile Bucky wore widened, and he slapped Jake on the shoulders again. "Glad to hear you're ready to go. Love the last of the season's training."

Jake wanted to let out a sigh of relief, feeling the

dampness under his arms and down his back. Even though it was warm out, he wasn't sweating from the heat, so he bit down hard on the inside of his cheek, holding it together. The last thing he wanted was to appear weak.

He felt he should say something, but what? He just couldn't get his tongue to connect with his brain. "Jeger looks good."

"Jeger looks like shit. He's become cautious. You can see he hesitates now, ever since he busted his ribs. I don't know. Some guys bounce back from an injury, but a few never shake it off. He's lost it. Maybe he'll never get it back. That's when you've got to know yourself. When your career's done, son, it's best you figure it out yourself without anyone telling you."

He didn't know what to say to that. It was a career burner, what Jeger had done, especially when he appeared to be on a downward slide. But then again, Jeger was one of the old guys, at thirty-two. He had been with the Cardinals for nine years, and when his contract was up, it wasn't likely to be renewed. A nightmare for any pro ball player.

"Last good year was two years ago, when he ran seven hundred and twenty-six yards on forty-six catches. You need to be quick, think fast, have agility—be smart, quick minded. Jeger's lost his edge. No, that position takes a different kind of mental sharpness, being fearless to race across the middle of the field on a third and ten and stretch out for a crossing route when you know you're going to get hammered, get hit hard by some guy who has thirty to forty pounds on you. And that's what you got, Jake Wilde."

Huh? That sure in the hell wasn't what he'd

expected. He'd never thought of himself as fearless. No, that was his brother Logan. There were still times when life scared the ever-living shit out of him and he found himself picking up the phone to call his brother. Jake just did things, especially in the game, without thinking about someone coming at him or who was coming up behind him. He caught the ball and ran, moved, and he could spin on a dime when the other team tried to take him out. So why, then, wouldn't Jill call him back? He gave his head a shake and pulled in a breath. He needed her out of his head so he could focus on the game.

He forced himself to remember every time he got hit… It had been hard, coming out of nowhere and taking him out, knocking the wind out of him. He had never seen it coming. It had done something to him, but Jake knew that was when he had to push himself hard to be better, faster. That was why he'd torn his ACL, pushing through a minor injury, not listening to his body when it was screaming to stop. He was thickheaded and persistent, and for the life of him, he couldn't figure out why he couldn't be like other guys and let things go. Jill still hadn't called. Damn, her image just wouldn't leave him be and get the hell out of his head. He fisted his hands.

"You don't say much, do you?" Bucky said.

This time, Jake faced him. This man, for the next three years in his contract, was the one person who would stand between him being benched and having the chance to show his stuff on the field. "I talk when I have something to say. So do you want me out there?"

The team doctor had cleared him. He was in great shape, having spent time every day in the gym, keeping every other part of his body primed and ready to go.

Bucky slid off his shades, and his deep hazel eyes took in Jake as if trying to figure him out. Good luck on that. Jake knew he was as open as he was going to be right now, still feeling burned and betrayed by the coach who'd meant everything to him, and then there was Jill.

"You got your stuff?" Bucky said, gesturing with his chin to the bag looped over Jake's shoulder. "Go get changed and get out there." He slapped Jake on the back and then walked away to where the Cardinals were training on the field.

This was his team, his new team. Maybe if he said it enough, he'd start to believe it. He took a breath and blew it out, then headed to the locker room to change. He would step out onto the field and train with a team that, to him, still wasn't his family.

He was sweaty and sore, and he could taste blood. He'd been tackled hard from behind, taken down by three of what he thought were the heaviest guys on the team. It was overkill. They had piled on him, and he heard something in his back crack as he moved his now stiffening shoulder. He knew he needed a rubdown to work all the kinks out. The blood in his mouth must have come from the last of the four poundings he'd taken—even though this was just practice and he'd had his mouthguard firmly in place. Evidently, this was his "welcome to the team" initiation. Or maybe payback for the last game he'd played against them with the Seahawks.

"Good practice, Wilde. Way to hold your own out there." Dorcel, the quarterback, caught up to him on the way to the locker room. His jet-black hair was damp and stuck to his head.

"Thanks, I guess." All he knew about Steve Dorcel was that he was one of the highest-paid quarterbacks in the NFL, married, with a kid on the way.

"You didn't miss once, and the guys really tested you."

Testing him, was that what they'd been doing? Jake was pretty sure it had been more. They were pissed he was there, moving in on Jeger's position, thinking he was there to replace him, which, he was pretty sure, was Coach's intent. Everyone knew it, but no one was saying it. Maybe that was why he felt they still saw him as the enemy.

"That's the name of the game, isn't it?" Jake said.

Dorcel pushed open the locker room door, paused, and smiled at Jake, one of those cocky smiles that said, just maybe, he wasn't feeling quite the same way as the others on the team. Then he walked in, listening to the catcalls and locker-room talk from the other players. Jake pulled open his locker, retrieved his bag, and set it on the bench behind him, then glanced at his cell phone resting on the shelf. Of course, he couldn't stop himself from reaching for it and checking again, as he had a hundred times already that day, just to make sure the ringer hadn't been turned off. His heart jumped just a little when he saw there were two missed calls and a message, and he felt the knot twist in his stomach again when he saw Jill's number.

Someone passing by patted his shoulder, but he didn't look over or say a word. He thumbed through the screen and checked the message, then pressed the phone to his ear. He had to walk to the door, as the noise in the locker room was too loud.

"Hi, Jake." He could hear something in Jill's voice on the message as she hesitated. His first thought was that he needed to find a way to go to her, to find out what was wrong. "I got your messages, and I'm sorry I didn't call you back. But, well, I just hope your move went well, and take care."

He realized she had hung up. That was it. What the fuck? She sounded off, maybe because of the distance. Had to be that something was wrong. He looked around the now empty hallway and dialed her number. It rang only once before he heard her sweet voice.

"Hi, Jake." She didn't sound like herself, but she had answered the phone, hallelujah.

"I just got your message. I was in practice or I would have picked up." He sounded like such a dork. She wasn't making this easy, but then, Jill wasn't much of a talker. Neither was he, but damn, he loved her, really loved her. "Are you all right? Because you don't sound all right."

"I'm sorry, Jake." Was she crying on the other end? "I miss talking to you."

"Hey, it's okay. Listen, I'm here, baby. I can have a ticket waiting for you at the airport, and you can get on the next plane. I'll take care of everything. Just come down here." And he would. He just needed to get her there, to hold her in his arms. He knew he could fix everything and anything for her. Then she'd know just how much she meant to him. It was all this damn distance, distance she'd put between them. She was confused, was all. He'd pushed too hard.

She sighed. "Jake, you're not listening to me."

He was trying to make out the background noise and figure out where she was. Soft music, maybe from a radio, and then he heard a door close and it was quiet. "Jill, where are you?" He pictured the apartment she'd moved her things out of, the one that was paid up until the end of the month. He knew she still had a key.

"I didn't want to get into this on the phone. You've been such a good friend. You were there for me, a shoulder to lean on. And I loved being with you, but I was kidding myself."

What the hell was she talking about? He didn't like the direction this was going. He'd done everything he could to protect her, to cherish her, the one thing his brother had never done. She had to know how much he loved her.

"Jill, whatever you're thinking, don't. Come down here. Let's sit down and talk this out. Having this distance between us isn't the answer. You're freaking out because I asked you to marry me, and maybe you're panicking a bit. Maybe it was too soon for you. I can wait, but you gotta know I'm all in for you. I love you."

"You're not hearing me, Jake. I don't love you."

He couldn't believe she was saying this, and his heart squeezed as the panic began to build. She was confused. There was no way a woman like her could hide the feelings she had for him when he was buried inside her so deeply. The way she responded to him, to his touch, his kiss, the look in her eyes and the way they brightened when she came around him…that wasn't a lie. That last time, before he asked her to marry him, he hadn't used any protection. Of course she knew, and maybe he was being selfish, wanting to bind her to him. Maybe he was a prick for doing it. He didn't want to look too closely at his motives. He may not have liked who he'd become, but he also knew, in that moment, he'd do it again in a second.

"Jill, maybe I pushed too hard." He rammed his fingers in his damp, disheveled hair. It was getting long and knotted. He pulled it away from his face hard.

"No, Jake. You made it easy for me, too easy, so easy that I didn't have to face up to my feelings. You have no idea how good it felt, you taking care of everything. You were my rock, my friend, and you deserve someone who can love you for the wonderful man you are. You have a lot to offer."

What the hell was she saying? "Jill, I want to give everything to you, to have a family with you, to be with you. We're so good together! I know you want me. You can't hide the reaction you had to me in bed. You can't fake that. Are you pregnant?" He had to know. Damn, he was such an asshole.

She didn't say anything, and that made the anxious knot that twisted in his gut tighten even more.

"Jill, answer me. You know the last night we were together, I wasn't prepared for you to walk out."

"No, you were trying to find a way to keep me. I figured it out after, when you asked me to marry you. It was then I realized it had gone too far. It was my wakeup call about how serious it was between us. I didn't mean for it to go there. I just wanted—"

"You wanted what?" The anger came out of nowhere. It burned as he felt his hold on her, them, disintegrating. He couldn't believe what she was saying.

"Don't be mad at me! I couldn't bear it, Jake. I miss you, but not in the way you think. I miss my friend Jake, who was there for me, who listened to me. You have such big, amazing, strong, broad shoulders, and the way you allowed me to lean on you… You made me feel so safe. But I can't, we can't, because I don't love you the way you love me. I can't love you like that no matter how much I wanted to. I really tried, told myself it was better for me because you're the better man. I'm not being fair to you…because I still have feelings for Samuel."

What the fuck? How could she, after what he'd done to her? He didn't know what to do with his hands. He wanted to hit something, someone, as he squeezed the phone. "Are you kidding me? Are you forgetting how he picked up another woman right in front of you because he was getting cold feet? His way of dumping you, and then he moved the chick in. He really didn't think very much of you, did he?" Now he was being an ass, a hurtful, spiteful ass, but he didn't care. The woman on the other end of the phone, the woman he loved, was jamming an icepick into his heart because…why? She was so fucked up because of his brother, the asshole who had a hold on her.

"I know what he did, and I hate him for that, but there's a fine line between love and hate, and Samuel has always been my everything. I just didn't know it until you asked me to marry you. I knew I would be settling with you, and I don't ever want to settle. That's not being fair to me, and that's not being fair to you. I love Samuel, not you."

"Where are you?" he asked again. He was out of his mind, and for a moment he wondered just how stupid he was. He was, right now, considering getting on a plane and going to see her so he could talk to her face to face. He knew if he just touched her, was with her in the same room, she'd realize she was kidding herself. Because the chemistry that clicked between them was so off the charts that she'd have to force herself to admit she was wrong. Yeah, that was it. She was just confused. He could forgive her for that.

"Jake, don't do this. You're making this so hard. You

need to look after yourself, and you have a new opportunity with your new team. You need to walk away from me, Jake. Go be the success I know you are."

"Jill, I'll come to you. We'll talk, you'll see—"

"Stop it, Jake!" she cried. "I don't want to hurt you anymore, but you're pushing too hard. You need to back off. I didn't want you to find out like this, but I'm with Samuel now. I'm staying with him, so don't call me again."

He was squeezing the phone, listening to the buzz of the disconnected line. Maybe it was shock or disbelief or something, because he felt lightheaded, as if the entire team had just jumped on him, knocking everything he believed to be true out of him. It was cruel, and he heard the words over and over again in his head. She was with his brother. It took a second before he realized that it wasn't just Jill who had screwed him but Samuel too.

He didn't think; he just reacted, throwing his phone into the concrete wall and watching as it shattered. "Fuck!" he roared as the knife plunged in him again. Betrayal. His brother was such an asshole.

"Whoa! I hope she was worth it."

He jumped at the feminine voice behind him. He turned around, staring into the bold, big blue eyes of one of the cheerleaders. She had a bag tossed over her shoulder and was wearing white shorts and a peach tank top. Her long hair, more mahogany than red, was tied back and hung down to her waist. She was slender with curves. She gestured to the wall where he'd just shattered his phone, and for a moment he felt like a busted idiot.

Crap! He hoped no one else had noticed, as he realized they were both standing in the open hallway of his new stadium. A great first impression this had made. He didn't want to be known as the crazy, stupid player who couldn't hold it together. As she took in the cell phone busted up on the concrete, sweat ran down his back.

"I'm Chris, and you're Jake Wilde, the new guy." She didn't reach out to shake his hand, just gripped the bag over her shoulder. Smart girl. Maybe she was scared, but the way she stood in front of him, taking him in, she didn't seem scared of anything.

"Sorry, that was just—uh…"

She held up her hand, stopping him from digging himself into a hole and looking like one of the biggest fools around. He pulled his hand over his face, feeling the dampness. "I wasn't eavesdropping, but from the one side I couldn't help but hear, sounds like you're having some girl trouble. I don't normally shove my nose in someone's business, but since it's just one of those days, I feel compelled to say from your outburst and pleading that you're wasting your time on someone who isn't interested in you, and that's a one-way street to getting yourself locked up, having a restraining order filed against you, or turning your life upside down and losing everything you've worked so hard for. Do yourself a favor and move on. Take my advice or not."

She turned and started to walk away, having just listened to him begging like a fool. Damn, he was embarrassed, furious.

"Hey, wait a minute."

She glanced over her shoulder at him but didn't turn back, this woman who'd just witnessed him at his worst.

"You're a cheerleader, right?"

She only blinked, and he wasn't sure she was going to answer.

"Sorry. Yeah, I'm Jake, the new guy. You said your name was Chris? Chris what?" He didn't know why, but he wanted to know her full name, who she was, maybe to somehow save his dignity.

He stepped forward and reached down for his shattered phone, then pulled in a breath and she looked away before lifting those blue eyes up to him. "Yes, one of the many cheerleaders. My name is Chris Jeger. Welcome to the team, Jake. You okay now?"

He wasn't sure whether she was mocking him or seriously asking. "As you said, just girl trouble," he replied. "Women can tie you up in knots. Chris Jeger, thanks. Any relation to Myles Jeger, wide receiver?"

She didn't blink, smile, nothing, so hard to read. "He's my brother," she said.

CHAPTER
Five

It was pathetic. Everything about the new guy who was there to push her brother out reeked of drama and chaos. Chris didn't know what had made her stop and watch him, considering she'd made her mind up to hate Jake Wilde before he got there, because he was coming in to take something that wasn't his. When she'd first heard the team was picking up his contract even after his recent injury, she'd hoped—no, prayed—that he'd be a liability for the team, at the same time cheering her brother on. She wasn't a fool. She'd heard the whispers that Myles Jeger was on his way out, that he'd lost his nerve. But she knew the truth: That wasn't what had happened. Busted ribs and injuries weren't enough to keep her brother down, not ever. There was something else going on.

She needed to talk to Myles. That was why she had been out in the hallway by the Cardinals' locker room, waiting, and had seen the new guy walk out. She knew she shouldn't have listened to what had surely been a very personal and private conversation. The new guy was pining for a woman, and it was absolutely, one hundred percent pathetic, considering it had taken her one second to figure out, from what had sounded like begging, that the girl didn't share his feelings. Pathetic. She'd recognized the desperation in his voice, though. Maybe that was why she'd been rather short with him, considering it hadn't been so long ago that she'd been in his place, crushed, gutted, just another fool.

But she wasn't about to stick around and converse with the enemy. She put one foot in front of the other, determined to put distance between herself and that kind of pathetic desperation. Chris made her way to the parking lot, seeing the cars and trucks, feeling the warmth of the sun, and then shut her eyes when she realized her car wasn't there because she'd caught a ride with another cheerleader. "Damn, come on, Chris, pull it together."

She stopped behind a red BMW, gripping the strap of her bag over her shoulder, and looked around for her brother's blue pickup. She'd just wait by his truck, and then they could have a much needed talk and she could figure out a way to get him to tell her what the hell was really going on.

"Come on, Myles, where did you park?" She lifted her hand to her forehead against the bright sun as she scanned the parking lot, but she couldn't see his truck. Maybe he had driven his Corvette, but that wasn't something he normally did for practice.

"Hello again."

She jumped when she heard the deep voice behind her and turned to see Jake Wilde, his hair still wet from showering, with his gym bag tossed over his shoulder. He looked good, wearing blue jeans, a light t-shirt across the span of his shoulders. His chest was ripped. She had a hard time looking away, but she made herself glance up into his dark shades.

"Hi," she said. For the life of her, she couldn't figure out what else to say. Where the hell was Myles?

He looked around over her head. "Were you looking for someone?" The way he said it, the way he was watching her, made her uneasy.

"Yeah, my brother. I caught a ride with one of the other cheerleaders and was going to hitch a ride back with Myles, but I don't see his truck." She looked over her shoulder, squinting into the bright sun, trying to spy his shiny red Corvette. "Or his car."

"He's gone already. Come on, I'll give you a ride." Jake was holding his keys, gesturing behind her. "I've got a rental until I get settled here."

He started walking toward a white Yukon SUV. He pressed a button on his keychain, and the doors unlocked with a beep. Chris wondered how her brother had slipped out so fast. She took one step and then another over to Jake as he opened the back of the SUV and tossed in his bag. He reached for hers, and for a second, she wondered whether this was a good idea. Maybe she should go back in and ask one of the other guys to drive her. She didn't know this guy, the new guy who was there to steal what her brother had worked so hard for. But instead, she handed him her bag so he could toss it in the back with his.

"You really don't mind? Because I'm out past Glendale."

He was shaking his head as he closed the hatch. "No, that's fine." Then he did the most unusual thing. He walked around to her side and opened the passenger door for her, even holding out his hand to help her in. A gentleman, wow. She'd thought that was a lost art. She hesitated a second. Unusual, really. What was this guy's deal?

He closed her door, and she watched as he walked around the front of the SUV and climbed in, sliding under the wheel. Maybe she was staring at him as he slid the key in the ignition, because he cleared his throat and said, "Seatbelt."

"Right." Of course, she reached for the seatbelt, feeling so damn awkward as she tried to figure him out. Her first impressions left her without a clue what he was about, and she couldn't help thinking again about the chick on the other end of the phone blowing him off. But then, she didn't know the whole story.

He backed out, his arm tossed around the back of her seat. His hand was large, the kind of hand that could do amazing things running over a woman's body. She could feel the heat, the chemistry, and made herself look away. What was it about these players that had women falling all over them like fools? It was as if they knew how to use the charm and play it up. She wondered if they were all the same. Chris had thought she was immune after Troy. Maybe this was chemistry, or maybe it was just the fact that she knew Jake was mentally taken by another woman. She was a sucker for them, the ones she had no hope in hell with because they were already committed to someone else.

"So what else do you do for work, Chris?" he asked, his voice deep, as he pulled out of the parking lot.

"I work at a small law firm. I'm a legal secretary."

He pulled one hand over his face with a scrape of whiskers. "That sounds interesting," he said, resting one hand on the wheel and the other against the door. She wondered if he really was interested or just being nice. Small talk and all those social niceties… She hated when people really didn't mean what they said. She couldn't tell with Jake, but she was sure he was distracted, probably thinking of that girl, the one he'd been pleading with on the phone. For a moment, she empathized with him, but she again reminded herself he was stealing something that didn't belong to him.

"Not really," she said. "Sometimes there are land disputes, family stuff. The lawyer I work for does mostly family law, you know, divorces, separations, custody battles. Always some drama walking in the front door. But she's nice, lets me work around my training practices." She rested her hand on the dark padded door and glanced at her fingers, her nails short and clipped. No polish.

She wondered if he was listening to her. Maybe not. He seemed so distracted, but then, she didn't really know him, only what she thought he would be like. Funny how some people turned out nothing like how she pictured them. He was only giving her a ride, though. And really, where the hell was Myles?

"So how do you like Phoenix?" she asked. She sucked at small talk. Guys usually carried the ball, but the moody guy driving her now didn't seem interested in creating any kind of conversation. This could be a really long drive, painful. She made herself glance out the window, wincing, wishing she'd said no to the ride.

"Don't know it. Haven't seen any of it other than my hotel last night and the field this morning. It's warm." He glanced her way. "How long have you lived here?"

"Five years. I moved from Texas after I finished my

GED. Stayed with Myles until I found a job. He hooked me up with the team for the cheerleading gig. I danced all through college, was a cheerleader in high school. I was excited when I got the position."

He didn't nod or anything. He either wasn't listening or was taking in everything she said. It was unnerving how he didn't respond at first. "You got family in Texas?" He was looking straight ahead, and she wondered if this was his small talk. Football guys were not known for being deep thinkers, or so she thought.

"Mom and Dad are in Houston, suburbia. Myles and I are it for the kids, a boy and a girl and they were done. You?" She wondered about Jake. What made him tick? Something nagged that she was being a traitor to her brother.

"Parents in Boise. Have four brothers, one still in Boise with his girlfriend. We were raised in Idaho. Joe and his second wife are still there where we grew up, in Post Falls—small, rural. Logan, my big brother, is a sheriff in McKay. He's there with his new family."

She didn't miss the way he hesitated. "That's three. Where's the other brother?"

His face appeared to darken, and she'd have been a fool to miss the tension that seemed to suddenly appear between them. He hesitated as she wondered what bad blood existed in his family.

"Samuel is in Seattle," was all he said, holding his jaw tight. He glanced over his shoulder to change lanes, speeding up.

"Seattle, that's where you were. Are you and your brother in Seattle close?" Maybe she should have left it alone.

He actually laughed, but it didn't sound friendly. "At

one time," he said. She was positive he was going to say more, but he just stopped talking.

"Bad blood there or something?"

He glanced over at her and then back to the road. "Curious, aren't you?" The way he said it, she felt she'd crossed a line into personal territory.

"Sorry. Call it an occupational hazard. I see a lot of people whose relationships are on the rocks. With love and hate, there's such a fine line, and sometimes the reason comes down to a misunderstanding."

"Misunderstanding…" he said under his breath, making a face. "No misunderstanding."

She just stared at him as he kept his gaze on the road and wiped his hand over his chin.

"I have an idea," he said. "Let's talk about you. So, tell me about yourself. You married, husband, kids, boyfriend?"

That was really getting to the point. "No, no, and no."

It was the first time he'd smiled since she met him. Maybe his icy exterior was starting to thaw. "Why not? Someone as gorgeous as you should have a hundred guys lining up in the wings to be with her."

"Yeah, well, that's the problem, isn't it? I'm not one of those girls who has guys lining up. I'm only interested in one."

And that one was Troy, who'd played right wing with the Cardinals but had been picked up by Denver. Her brother had warned her off the players, but she hadn't listened, and she'd been crushed when he up and left without her. The hazards of working too closely with the team.

"Sounds like there's someone there—or was?"

"There was. Now there's not."

He was watching her.

"He left," she said.

"Fool."

She swallowed past the ache that always built when she thought of losing Troy. It would have been one thing if she'd realized there was no future, but she'd believed he was the one. She'd never been so head over heels with anyone to the point that she couldn't let it go. She'd been obsessed, tried to tell herself he loved her still, that he really did want her. When would the hurt finally go away?

"You okay?" He actually reached across and touched her hand. The touch was unexpected, and she fisted her hand as she pulled it away and rested it in her lap. There it was, that awkwardness again.

She'd be damned if she'd let her vulnerability and weakness slip through. So she did what she always did when the situation called for it: She put on her game face. "Yeah, fine. Again, this is real nice of you to give me a ride." Damn, that really did sound pathetic.

"You hungry?" he said. She glanced over to him. He was looking her way, then glanced back to the road. "I mean if you don't have plans right now, would you like to stop for a bite to eat? I'm starved and hate eating alone. Don't have any friends here, so you'd be doing me a favor."

She just stared, knowing she needed to make an excuse, have him drop her off. He glanced her way again, and she opened her mouth to say no. "All right," she said. "There's a pretty great little Italian diner not far from my place. Makes the best pasta and fish."

"Sounds great. You just saved me from ordering room service and eating alone."

"Well, far be it from me to let you eat alone."

When he glanced her way again, with an easy smile that just touched his lips, she felt her heart do a little leap. And she made herself look away, because she also knew Jake was the enemy, and a football player, and this could only turn out very, very badly.

Six

What had he been thinking, asking this cute little redheaded cheerleader out to eat? It wasn't a date. Of course it wasn't a date, because Jake Wilde, in his mind, was still taken. His heart belonged to a woman who'd just dumped him in a Dear John sort of way over the phone. He'd had no time to process any of the phone call that had just taken all his hopes and dreams and flushed them down the toilet. And worse, his brother Samuel had just stabbed him in the back, again.

Right now, he hated the brother he had once loved so much. They'd been best friends, closer than most, and always together out on the town in Seattle. They even lived close to each other so they could do anything and everything together, even just hanging out with a beer or two or having a night out. But not now, not anymore.

He followed Chris into the quaint little Italian restaurant with red checked tablecloths and pictures of famous dead actors on the walls.

He hadn't missed the ass on this girl. She had one

fine set of buns, a slim waistline, and when she walked, she did it with her head held high. Her hair…he found himself noticing how different it was from Jill's: longer, redder, and thicker. This girl was a knockout and a nice distraction.

A portly man at the door smiled brightly at Chris. "Hey, how are you? Where's your brother?" He was Italian, gray haired, probably in his sixties. He glanced up at Jake curiously with a flash of something mischievous in his blue-gray eyes.

"Not sure," Chris said. "This is Jake Wilde, the new wide receiver for the Cardinals. Showed up just in time for the end of the season. We're here for a late lunch, if you're still serving?"

Jake wondered as he took in the empty restaurant. It was small, with maybe twenty tables, and not a soul in sight.

"Of course, for you," the man said. "Come on, I have a nice table by the window, and I think there's still some of Rosa's special grilled halibut with linguine." He guided them over to a table by the window and put a menu in front of them. "Can I get you something to drink to start, a glass of vino or beer?"

"Diet coke for me," Chris said as she glanced up from her menu.

"Water, please," Jake said, although he would've preferred a beer.

Chris was staring at her menu when the man left them.

"Nice place. The food good?" Jake asked, but if the spicy aroma wafting from the kitchen was anything to go by, the food was going to be mouthwatering. Damn, he was starving.

"The best—and I'm not kidding about that. I'm a foodie and have always said there's too many really good restaurants out there to waste your time on the ones that are just average, you know?" She shut her menu and rested her hands on the table. He hadn't even had a chance to look at the menu when the waiter returned with their drinks.

"Are you ready?" he asked.

"Jake?" Chris prompted him. "I know what I want."

"What are you having?"

"Caesar salad." She glanced up at the waiter, who frowned down at her and tsked.

"Your brother would make you order more than that. How about some meatballs?" he said, speaking to her like a father would. Jake wondered how well Chris knew him.

"Order her the meatballs, too, and I'll have the special," Jake said. "The halibut's good?"

The waiter kissed his own fingers in reply. "You'll love it." He scooped up the menus and left.

When Jake glanced across the table, he realized Chris was frowning up at him. "Everything okay?"

"Why did you order meatballs for me? All I wanted was a salad. You overstepped a bit, don't you think? I do have a mind of my own and can think for myself." She crossed her arms and leaned back in her chair.

He lifted both his hands in surrender. "You're right. Apologies, sorry. Just figured you can't live on lettuce. Don't worry. If you can't eat it, I'll finish it."

"I also can't eat like a football player or I'll be two hundred pounds."

He couldn't help smiling at her comeback. "You look pretty good from here," he said. She lifted her gaze to him, and he suddenly felt awkward. Time to change the subject. "So, Chris, what do you do for fun?"

She stretched out her foot and bumped his leg. "Sorry." She pulled it back, and he sensed a lingering awkwardness.

"Yeah, I'm a big guy," he said. "Take up my share of space and then some."

She had a lovely smile that showed off straight white teeth. He hadn't noticed before, but she had a mole on the side of her lip that he found extremely attractive. Her face wasn't painted with all that goop many women plastered on their skin. She looked clean and wholesome. Her eyes were like nothing he'd ever seen before. The blue…he'd swear a man could get lost in them. She cleared her throat, but he didn't look away. He was staring, but he liked what he was looking at.

"Movies, old ones," she said.

"Pardon?"

"You asked what I do for fun. I like old movies, the classics, Jimmy Stewart, Rock Hudson, John Wayne."

Well, that he hadn't expected. "Seriously, no bars, clubs, dancing, biking?" He didn't know why he was picturing her in a short skirt and a crowded club, dancing.

"Not much into the party scene. Would rather rent one of those old movies and sit and watch with a tub of popcorn. That's a night of fun for me. What about you, Jake?" she asked.

Of course, his head went right to his nights with Jill. Before that, he had always stopped in at a pub for some dancing, hoping to meet the one or just have a night of fun. "Not much, as of late," he said. He patted his pocket, about to check his phone, when he realized he couldn't because it was shattered in the trash bin outside the locker room.

Chris seemed to follow where his hand went as if she knew. She didn't say anything, but he still felt he needed to explain himself.

"My phone, I feel lost without it. I'll have to find a store around here to replace it."

She didn't even blink as she watched him. "You know, this may be none of my business, and I wasn't eavesdropping."

He wondered if he should call her out. Instead of leaving, she'd even stuck around to give him unwanted advice.

"Of course you were," he said. "I guess I wasn't really quiet, but didn't expect anyone to be standing out there."

"I was waiting for my brother, who must have slipped out before you, but yeah, you're right. I couldn't help hearing," she said.

Her arms were crossed, and he took in the way she pulled in a breath. "You must think I'm pretty pathetic, then," he said. He tapped his fingers on the table, and her eyes widened as she leaned across. Reaching out, she touched his hand.

"No, I don't think you're pathetic. I was thinking it wasn't so long ago that I was in your position, and I wouldn't wish that on anyone. It's like being kicked when you're down, like a puppy." She pulled her hand away and leaned back, and for a moment, he'd have sworn he saw some vulnerability, a hurt that was still raw and very real. Then it was gone and her game face was back on.

"Well, still, she was my brother's girlfriend," Jake

finally said. "Maybe I should have known better, but he got cold feet and picked up another woman in a bar in front of her. She dumped him, and, well…" What could he say? He'd always carried a torch for Jill. He'd envied his brother. He'd made himself available. Logan had been right about that, too. He'd loved the fact that she'd turned to him.

"Ouch. Let me guess, she leaned on you, cried on your shoulder, and you were there to pick up the pieces of her broken heart." She glanced away, watching something out the window as she rested her elbow on the table, her chin in her palm, before glancing back his way. "No, that just makes you human. Her, though, that's another story."

He didn't know what to make of Chris. "So what happened for you?"

She leaned back, wagging her finger at him. "No, we're talking about you and…" She hesitated, her brow knitting, and the blue of her eyes flashed with something he didn't think he could possibly tire of looking into. There was something in the way she looked at him that was nothing like Jill. Damn, he needed to get her out of his head.

"Jill is her name. I asked her to marry me, and…" He couldn't finish. He couldn't tell anyone what he'd done, trying to get her pregnant to tie her to him. Even though he wouldn't have admitted it before now, that was exactly what he'd been trying to do: make her love him, force her to stay with him. It stung to realize it, but it also hurt that she was so head over heels in love with his prick of a brother.

"She's not over your brother? She panicked, maybe had a reality check, and started backing away after she realized you weren't on the same page as her, not willing to be just a momentary distraction."

Boy, she was spot on. He leaned back, and then the waiter appeared with their meal, setting it in front of them. For a few minutes, they just ate in silence, and he stifled a smile when she dug into her meatballs. Maybe she was hungry after all.

"So how did you know that's what she did?" he asked. "I mean, I'm still trying to figure it out. I offered her everything, wanted to give her the world, security, family." *Love.* He'd just wanted to love her, for her to love him. "And she left. I haven't seen her in months."

"You've been calling, I take it, waiting by the phone for her to call you back, pushing, trying to change her mind, being understanding? Too understanding, willing to sell yourself short and settle on any crumb she'll toss your way. And all the while, you're eating your heart out," she said between mouthfuls. There was a dot of sauce at the side of her mouth, and he wanted to reach over with his finger and wipe it away. Chris must have known, as she reached for her napkin and wiped her mouth.

"Sounds like we're talking about more than me," he replied, gesturing with his fork toward her. He then wound it in the fresh pasta and shoved a forkful into his mouth, the garlic and fresh herbs coming alive on his tongue. She was right. The food was really good, and he didn't want his disaster of a love life shoved in his face anymore. He needed to shut up about Jill.

"Been there, made a fool of myself," she said. "Thought he cared more than he did. He left, and I kept calling, you know…" She trailed off. "Did she ask you not to call?" Damn, she had spun it right back to him.

"She said she needed space. I wanted to convince her otherwise, thought she was just freaking out because I popped the question. Never expected her to just disappear. Thought she'd come back."

Chris shook her head. "She told you she didn't know what she wanted, didn't she?"

He nodded. Maybe she did understand. "Yeah, something like that."

"How many messages did you leave before she called you back?"

He didn't want to tell Chris, as he thought about it now, because he'd lost count. Way too many times, and he'd just kept making excuses. When he loved someone with everything he had, Jake couldn't just let that person walk away. "Probably one too many."

"You do know there's a line you can't cross, and you may not even be aware of it. Sometimes it helps to have someone else point it out to you, because when you're emotionally in it, you can't see the road ahead. You're lost in this haze, you know? Doing stupid things, acting on emotion, calling and calling even if they don't call back. You make excuses for it, like maybe they were busy, didn't hear the phone or see the fifteen messages. So I'm telling you, because I've been there, my advice is to walk away. You called, she blew you off. She doesn't want to be bothered, and she's telling you you're done by ignoring you."

"So answer me this: Why do women always go back to the guys who treat them like shit?"

A slow, sad smile drifted across her face. "Because at the time, we're so in it that we don't realize we're just repeating the same patterns over and over. We go back to what we know even though it may not be what's best for us. A woman with a broken heart who's still reeling from betrayal isn't anyone you should be getting involved with. She needs time to heal, figure things out, get her head on straight. Rebounds never work, so when you put yourself in the picture, became a shoulder for her to cry on, of course she fell right into you. But her heart was still with your brother. You were just making it easier for her when she needed to figure her shit out."

"Well, she's with him now."

She shut her eyes and shook her head. "I'm sorry, Jake. I hate to say this to you, but you gotta know there's no future with a girl like that. Coming between you and your brother, she had to know. Of course she knew. That's shitty. Shame on her."

For a moment, his instinct was to defend Jill, but when he opened his mouth, the words fell away. "She may be pregnant."

"Oh." Chris paused with her fork in midair. "Yours?" She gestured with her fork, then forked up some salad.

He felt his face warm and was glad she looked away. Of course it would be his, wouldn't it? If she was pregnant. She hadn't denied it. He couldn't figure out what to say as he gestured to her. "Yeah, which has me tearing my hair out, because I don't understand her silence."

"Oh, Jake, take my advice or not, but I'm going to give it anyway. Walk away. It sounds like a very messy situation that could divide your family. I don't know your family or your brother, or this girl, but there isn't anything you can do. She's walked away, avoided your calls. That's the coward's way of saying, 'Get lost.'" Chris lowered her gaze to her plate and pushed her half-eaten salad away. "Done?"

"Yeah," he replied, shoving the last bite of pasta in his mouth. Instead of feeling good after talking with Chris, he felt like crap. He had some hard thinking to do. The last thing he wanted was anyone telling him to walk away from Jill. Damn, if she was pregnant, it would be his kid. She had to know he wanted this baby.

She started to reach into her bag.

"No, I got this," he said, pulling his wallet from his back pocket and lifting out cash, more than enough to cover the bill. He stood up. "Ready?"

She bit her lip as she stood, and he didn't know what to make of her expression. What was she thinking? Maybe he'd said too much, as Chris started out of the restaurant ahead of him. Then she stopped, and for a moment, he was positive she was about to say something else. But her smile was gone, and her expression had turned serious. She pulled open the door and walked out.

Jake turned back to the waiter, who lifted his hand to him and said, "Say hi to Myles."

Jake only nodded, thinking of the wide receiver he didn't know. He couldn't shake the feeling that his life was suddenly going in a direction he had no control over. That was something that had always unsettled him.

CHAPTER
Seven

The funny thing about soul-searching was the incredible ache that went along with it. Some of what Chris had said to him over lunch, despite the fact that he hadn't wanted to hear it, had stuck with him, and he couldn't help but be grateful to her. After their lunch had come a coffee and chat after practice the next day. She really was a breath of fresh air, and he had realized the night before in one of his dark, lonely waking hours that she'd been the best sounding board he'd ever had. He barely knew her, but she was an unlikely friend who had come out of left field, a great listener, one he had never expected to find.

Maybe that was because of her own experience, something he suspected still haunted her. He'd yet to get her to talk about what made her understand him so well. He wondered who it was that had hurt her so badly. Something about the ending of personal relationships was especially devastating. And he realized that was what it was. She understood what he was feeling. Jake couldn't help but envy those who could just shake it off and move on, only he wasn't made that way. He'd never been able to get over it. He held on to things, reliving them over and over in his head. Maybe that was why he continued to pine away for a woman he wished he could stop thinking about.

He glanced at his phone again as he walked out of the hotel gym with a towel around his neck, sweaty, and pushed the button to the elevator. He glanced up to the light indicating the floor and then over to the front desk. The blonde behind it was looking his way. There it was, a smile and a wave. The elevator dinged.

"Have a good day," he said as he stepped inside. He really needed to figure out a place to live. Today, maybe.

He leaned against the back wall after punching the button to the fourteenth floor and watching the doors slide closed, then let out a heavy sigh, bored with the four walls of his hotel.

When his cell phone rang, he stood straight, and his heart thumped once, twice. He ran his hand over his damp hair and put the phone to his ear. "Jill…"

There was a pause on the other end. "Uh, no. This is your brother, Logan."

He thunked his head against the mirror at the back of the elevator. Idiot, what the hell was the matter with him? Every time the phone rang, he couldn't stop hoping Jill had had a change of heart and was calling him. He was glad no one was there to witness how pathetic he was. He looked up to the corner, the security camera he knew was watching everything.

"Hey, Logan, how are you?" Jake was distracted and tired, having worked himself so hard that his muscles ached. But he was convinced that was the only way he could keep his sanity. His mind continued to work overtime.

"Um, good, but I'm calling about you. Haven't heard from you in a while. Called you a few days ago, left you a message. You didn't call back."

Right. When he was having coffee with Chris, he'd silenced the call when he'd seen Logan's name on the screen, not wanting to talk to his big brother, not when his heartache was so raw, because Logan would know, and he'd pry and keep at him until he spilled. The Jill thing was really messing with him, and he felt like such a fool. He didn't want anyone telling him, "I told you so." Chris never once had said that to him.

"Yeah, I, uh…" He couldn't come up with a lie that would be believable.

"You're not talking to anyone anymore?" Logan asked. Just like his brother to cut right to it.

"Sorry, just a lot on my mind. How's Julia, the twins, and the baby?"

"Great. Julia says hi. The girls would love to see you. You got time off now. Isn't the season almost up? You have holidays, don't you, before the summer training camp starts?"

Jake had to roll his shoulders, because it seemed his brother was keeping track of him. "No can do. Got to find a place here and get out of this hotel." The elevator dinged and the doors slid open to his floor, and he stepped out, taking in the dark brown carpet and off-white walls. "Not sure how long it will take me to find a place." A condo, an apartment, something closer to the stadium and out of the downtown area.

"Well, after you find a place, why don't you come up for a visit, spend a couple weeks with us?"

At any other time, he would've loved to visit Logan and his family. He'd always gone to Logan when he was in trouble, because Logan had been the one constant for him, growing up. But not this time. There was something so hairy about this mess, this bitch of a triangle with Jill and Samuel, that he didn't want anyone taking sides, and he didn't think he could quietly sit at his brother's house without talking about Jill. So he had decided to take himself out of the equation and stay away until he could…what? Figure out a way to get her out of his head.

"I think I'm going to stay here for the time being, get settled, find a place, you know, but thanks for the offer."

"Thanks for the offer? Seriously, Jake, this is me you're talking to. Just what the hell's going on with you?" There he was, the bossy big brother he couldn't blow off.

"Nothing, Logan. There's nothing for you to worry about. I'm in a new place, a new city, with a new team, trying to find my footing and get settled." He shoved his keycard in his door and walked into the freshly made-up room, taking in the king-size bed, the flat-screen TV on the wall, and the small table with two chairs by the window. It was an average hotel room with all the amenities and nothing else. He really did need to find his own place.

"Would this be the same 'nothing for me to worry about' that I heard from Samuel?"

Samuel, the person who had Jake fisting his hand and gritting his teeth so hard he was positive his jaw cracked. Samuel was the last person he wanted to talk about.

"Leave it alone, Logan. Samuel's not my favorite

topic right now." He sat on the white duvet and leaned over to untie his sneakers, then kicked them off, pulling the towel from around his neck and tossing it on the bed. He pulled off his sweaty socks and threw them to the floor. He needed a shower, and he needed to get off the phone and away from Logan's fifty questions.

"What happened with Jill?" He really wasn't going to leave it alone, and Jake should've known that. He should tell him just enough that he could get off the damn phone and in the shower and then get back to his brooding.

"What do you want me to say, Logan? You were right. I fucked up. I haven't seen Jill since before Christmas, after I asked her to marry me. I apparently pushed too hard, and she wasn't ready. She said she needed space. I thought I gave it to her, but then it dragged on and on. I called, and apparently, she's back with Samuel. What more can I say?" Maybe that was enough that Logan would leave it alone and stop asking.

"Well, shit," Logan said. Jake heard some muffled curses, and he pulled the phone away and stared at it for a second.

"I take it Samuel didn't tell you Jill's with him," Jake said. He didn't know why he wanted to know, but he did. It was like pouring acid in a gaping wound. The morbid curiosity would be his downfall, just like slowing down to get a better look at a roadside accident. Logan had to know, and for a moment, Jake wanted to ask him about Samuel and Jill, how she was doing, where they were, but he was afraid of knowing they were happy, that she was happier without him.

"No, but I knew something was up with both of you. I was worried—am worried. Someone coming between two brothers, my brothers…it's not okay, Jake. She shouldn't be with either of you."

He wanted to yell at Logan that she belonged with him, that he was right for her, that she was a perfect fit for him. He wasn't ready for anyone to tell him that they didn't belong together. His wounds were still fresh, and he wondered when he would be able to get through the day without her image popping into his mind every five or ten minutes. It was exhausting, maddening. Chris was who he wanted to talk to.

"Jake, is there anything I can do?" Logan sounded as tired as he was.

"No." He wished there was. He wished a lot of things, but he didn't know what the right thing to hope for was anymore.

"I want to say don't worry, that it will get better. Heartache sucks big time, but family is everything, Jake. You need to talk to Samuel. You two can't let this come between you. You can't let Jill come between you."

"Well, sorry to disappoint you, Logan, but she already has. And that's all on Samuel."

Logan sighed on his end, then growled in frustration. Jake recognized the sound well and was positive that if Logan had been in the same room as him now, he'd have taken his shoe and smacked him upside the back of the head. It was something he had done a few times, and it made Jake feel as if he were just a kid, screwing up.

"I know you, Jake, maybe better than you know yourself. You're hurting, and you feel betrayed. But you need to ask yourself something. How long were you in love with your brother's girlfriend before he pulled that dumbass move, and then you swooped in like a knight on a white horse to rescue her? You were just biding your time, loving her from afar. I didn't realize it until now, but you walked into this with your eyes wide open. You coveted your brother's girlfriend, Jake. You should know better."

He couldn't believe Logan was saying what he wouldn't admit to himself. It made him sound like such an asshole, and he wasn't. But then, listening to Logan and the way he put it, he sounded pathetic, as if he were the one responsible for his broken heart.

"That's not fair, Logan. It just kind of happened." *Bullshit.* He shut his eyes. He couldn't even make himself believe it had been okay anymore. What Samuel had done was wrong, and Jill had walked right into Jake's arms.

"Jake, Samuel has always been a prick with women. I'm not saying what he did was okay. He treated Jill like crap, and he was a scumbag for doing that. But you crossed a line when you started up with her. Being a shoulder to cry on is one thing, but what did you think was going to happen when you consoled her? I mean, you're not chopped liver. Take a look in the mirror. You have women falling all over you, wanting to be with you, and you take a woman who's vulnerable and hurt and in love with your brother who has just kicked her to the curb? Of course she fell into bed with you. It was never going to work. It couldn't have. Call your brother. Work it out with him. You should never have slept with her. You should never have crossed that line."

"Don't lecture me, Logan. It happened. And no, I'm not going to call him." He shook his head as if Logan could see him, but he was thousands of miles away in another state. For the first time, Jake needed distance from his family and everyone he knew. "Listen, I've got to go. I need to shower, and then I have to call a realtor to look at some places. Stop worrying about me and this Jill thing. It's a moot point. She's back with Samuel."

Logan let out a heavy sigh again. "Fine, but we're not done talking about this."

"Later," was all he said before hanging up and tossing his cell phone on the bed. He pulled off his damp t-shirt and threw it on the dresser, then walked into the small bathroom, flicked on the shower, and looked at his image in the mirror, wondering why Jill had walked out the door.

After showering, he changed into a pair of jeans and a yellow t-shirt, his hair brushed back, tucked behind his ears. It was getting long enough that he could probably tie it back, or maybe he should find a barber and get it cut. He glanced in the mirror at his face and the five-day beard starting to grow. He could probably add an earring, a diamond stud, and change his image from stable, dependable Jake to reckless bad boy. The thought, for a minute, seemed appealing. It was a good idea, one he was seriously considering, but as he pulled his hand over his face, he wondered what Jill would think.

"Damn it, Jake, get her out of your head," he said as he strode out of the bathroom and flicked off the light, taking in the cramped hotel room. "Yeah, you need to find a place today."

Because if he didn't, these four walls would likely start closing in on him, more so than they already were.

CHAPTER

Eight

S he should have been watching where she was going, head down in her pencil skirt, blazer, and pumps as she hurried from the courthouse where she'd just picked up the divorce decree for one of their clients. She clutched the envelope, wondering how the courier could have forgotten. Her feet were starting to ache. Was this the first time? No. How many times in the past week alone? Four. Damn, she didn't have time for this.

She bumped into someone's large chest. Hands grabbed her shoulders when she lost her balance, and she dropped the envelope, her glasses knocked sideways.

"Whoa, there. Are you okay?"

She pushed up her glasses, and her heart thudded, because she would've known his voice anywhere. Chris looked up to Jake Wilde, who released her shoulders and lifted his stylish black shades to reveal amazing blue eyes filled with humor. Did he ever look good! His dark hair was brushed back, and she loved the rough unshaved look, especially when it surrounded full lips that she imagined would be absolutely sinful to kiss. Damn, the girl he pined for was an idiot. She realized he was frowning.

"Is that you, Chris? Didn't know you wore glasses." Was that amusement that tugged at his lips?

"Sorry, I wasn't looking," she said. "How are you?" She swallowed and let him squat down to pick up the envelope.

"Didn't recognize you," he said. "Cute."

She wondered whether his smile was his game face or genuine. She'd had enough practice using hers, but she didn't know Jake well enough to know whether he too had a flashy, practiced smile. Coffee and lunch or not, she still didn't know if she was just a distraction or if he was real.

She pushed the dark-rimmed glasses up her nose again when they slipped down. "I usually wear contacts, except at work, so this is my work persona." She took the envelope from him. "Thank you. Have to get this back to the office. Just picked it up at the courthouse, and I was trying to hurry. I have a ton of work and didn't have time for this. Courier forgot to pick it up."

She was rambling. He lifted the envelope, and she didn't know why she felt so damn awkward. Maybe it was because she was thinking of her boss, Jennifer, at the law office, who worked endless hours and expected the same of her.

He looked over his shoulder, down the street, then back to her. "Are you walking?"

"Running, actually, just a few blocks from here to the office. I need to drop this off and file a few things, and then I'm done for the day."

Of course, his gaze went right to her pumps, his eyebrows rising in amusement. "Runnin' in heels, impressive. Why don't I walk with you, since you're probably the only friendly face I know here in Phoenix?" There, he did it again, smiled, and her heart gave a little hiccup. Bad, bad idea. He was in love with someone else, and she didn't come second to anyone.

"Sure." Why had she said that? She could hear the lecture coming in her head, so she shut it down and started walking. Jake was right beside her, and he put his hand on the small of her back to move her around some corporate suit who almost walked into her, glued to his phone, texting away. It felt so good. Dammit, that was not a good thing.

"So what are you doing down this way?" she asked. She realized he had slowed down to walk with her, another gentlemanly gesture. Friends, they were only friends, she reminded herself.

"Looking at some places to live, apartments, but they weren't really what I was looking for. Hey, you don't want to tag along, do you? I have a couple condos to look at next and wouldn't mind another opinion, another set of eyes."

She should say no, go home and lock the door and stay far, far away from Jake Wilde. After all, her heart was still smarting from her own failed relationships. "Why not? Let me just drop these off and grab my things."

"Great. Will give me a chance to see where you work. A big law firm, small one? Don't think you told me."

She glanced up to him and then back to the twelve-story building. So he had remembered. She gestured with her envelope, hearing the click of her heels. "Gabel and Sons, but there are no sons left, and Gabel Sr. is retired, leaving just his daughter, Jennifer, to run the show. It's right here." She gestured to the double doors.

Jake reached around her and pulled one open. The elevator was crowded, and Jake followed her to the office on the eighth floor, where Jennifer was on the phone with a client, she thought. She gave a light tap on the door and held up the envelope, and Jennifer, her dark hair in a ponytail, cigarette dangling from her lips, waved her in and let the phone slide from her mouth.

"Here it is," Chris said.

"Hey, thanks, Chris. You have a chance to type up the Anderson will, those changes they wanted?" Jennifer gripped the envelope and put out her cigarette, and Chris had to fight the urge to cough, knowing her boss only smoked when she was stressed.

"First thing tomorrow," she said. "Sorry, can't stay late."

"Practice?" She knew Jennifer was fishing, hoping to get her to work late.

"Something like that. See you tomorrow." She strode out of her boss's office and out to her desk, where Jake was taking in the earth tones of the small one-woman firm.

"Done?" he said.

She pulled open her bottom drawer and retrieved her bulky black purse. "Yeah, let's go."

He walked ahead of her and opened the door for her, letting her out first. "I parked around the corner. Was actually on my way back to my truck when I ran into you. At least now I know where you work." He glanced down at her pumps, the three-inch heels her feet were starting to ache from. "You okay to walk a few blocks in those?"

"Right as rain. I'm a girl who loves heels. I have no problem walking a few more blocks."

There was that smile again.

It was really hot outside, and she was glad she'd worn her white sleeveless blouse and left her legs bare. She could feel him watching her as they walked. It had been a long time since someone made her feel special or wanted.

"Your boss trying to get you to stay?"

She glanced up to him as he touched her arm and gestured to his SUV. "Always. I just learned to say no after a few times when she didn't pay me for the extra hours, saying salary means just that, and it's not hourly. That was enough of a wakeup call, because although I don't mind working overtime, I will not work for free. At least there I held my ground. Four o'clock, I'm done."

Jake said nothing as he opened the door for her, touching her elbow as he helped her in. She slid onto the leather seat and pulled her door closed, watching Jake walk around the front of his SUV to the driver's side. The girl he was still pining over was such an idiot.

"So where to first?" she asked, unable to think of what to say when he started the SUV.

He pulled out into traffic, driving with ease, a man in control behind the wheel. He lifted a folded paper from the console and held it out to her between his fingers. "There are two condo listings there. The realtor is meeting me at four thirty a few blocks from here. The other is across town. Would be a commute, but she says it's worth it. We'll see. So how have you been since I saw you last?"

Small talk. Damn, she hated that. "Good, I'm good. You?"

"Great." He didn't add anything.

This was going to be awkward. She wanted to ask about the girl who had him so twisted up inside, but at the same time, she didn't want to know. "So we're just two lost souls looking for a place for you to live."

He actually smiled, something genuine. He had a really nice smile. "Sums it up for me but not you, Chris." He shook his head. "You know, I'm glad I ran into you. You really are a breath of fresh air."

"Well, I try to be."

He slowed down and signaled, looking out her side. "I think this might be it."

Chris checked the address on the paper and noted the big block lettering on the side of the condo building. It was concrete and glass, nice. There was even a valet out front. "Wow, looks nice from the outside."

Jake pulled up in front and parked. "Sure does," he said before climbing out. He said something to the valet as Chris opened her door and reached for her purse, then stepped out. Jake's hand was on the door, and the way he was looking down at her had her feeling as if she really mattered.

"This is it," he said. "Apparently the realtor's already here."

She squeezed the strap of her purse as he closed the door behind her, and a doorman pulled the door to the building open. Jake was right behind her. She felt the touch of his hand on her lower back as they strode into marble and black glass, a little dated but nice.

"So what floor is it?" She looked up to him as he reached around and pushed the button for the bank of elevators

He had pulled off his sunglasses and tucked them

into the neck of his plain t-shirt. But there was nothing about his t-shirt and jeans that was ordinary. He didn't just look good; he made the ordinary look amazing. He held up his phone as if reading something. "Eighteen."

She only nodded when he didn't look away. Damn, he had amazing eyes. Kind, definitely not the flirty, shallow looks she was used to from the players. Her heartbeat kicked up. He wasn't smiling, and the look he gave her was too damn serious as the tension spiked. She wondered for a second whether he would kiss her. She squeezed the strap of her purse, feeling her palms sweat and her glasses slip down again, just as the elevator dinged. And just like that, the spell was broken.

"Shall we?" was all he said as he gestured to the empty elevator.

Chris made herself pull in a breath as she stepped inside, and as Jake pressed the button for the eighteenth floor, she had to remind herself that he was pining for another woman, and he was there to take her brother's spot.

Jake really wasn't in the mood to look at yet another place, but nothing he'd seen had screamed "This is it!" They had been livable, nice. He realized now how much he despised apartment hunting. As Chris was talking to the realtor, he looked out the floor-to-ceiling window, and Jill's image came out of nowhere, sucker-punching him. For a moment, he'd found it hard to breathe, thinking of her, picturing her there with him as he walked into the master bedroom. She would have loved the view, looking out at the skyline he was staring at right now.

A warm hand touched his arm. Chris. She was so damn cute in those glasses, the corporate getup and heels. She was frowning at him.

"You okay?"

What was he supposed to say? *Yeah, I was having fun with you when Jill snuck into my thoughts.* He shrugged. "Just realized how much I hate house hunting."

"Well, you haven't said two words to the realtor. You know you're the one looking, not me. I can keep talking, but you're the one who has to sign the lease and say you'll take it."

He didn't know why his chest felt tight. Maybe it was the thought of going back to an empty hotel room, the four walls. He didn't think he could do it for one more night.

"Come on, this one is nice, right?"

He turned around, taking in the light colors of the empty room. It was all earth tones, fifteen hundred square feet, with a nice walk-in kitchen, two full bathrooms, and underground parking. "Better than the last. Why would someone put carpet in the bathroom?" That had been the one thing preventing him from saying yes to the last one. He felt his moodiness setting in.

"Well, it was furnished. Didn't you say you wanted furnished?"

He wasn't sure if that was amusement or she was just teasing him. Damn, she really made him feel good. That wasn't something a woman had done in a really long time. He realized the realtor was watching them from the kitchen, a really nice kitchen, likely a chef's dream.

"So what do you think, Jake?" the realtor said. What was her name again, Loretta? She had jet-black hair, tall and slender, and a smile pasted to her lips that did nothing for him. "I know this one is a little farther away than you wanted, but isn't it stunning?"

He wondered if he was frowning when Chris touched his arm again. He turned away from the realtor and looked down at her.

"Come on, Jake," she said. "Look at this view, the floor-to-ceiling windows with a perfect view of the sunset. You have to admit the kitchen is nice, and there's the private gym downstairs, the lap pool…"

"Yeah, yeah, yeah, I get it. The bedrooms are huge, the walk-in steam shower, the heated floors… It's really nice, but it's not furnished. Wasn't planning on going furniture shopping. That puts me how many more nights in the hotel?"

She rested her hand on his arm again and gave a tug, pulling him across the creamy white carpet, which he could smell had been freshly steam cleaned, into the open kitchen past the realtor, who stepped out to the living room, maybe to give them some privacy. "Look, think of it this way: If you like the place, take it, and then buy the furniture and everything you need the way you want it instead of someone else doing it for you. The last one, as you pointed out, was older, and I'm pretty sure the bathroom carpet was the dealbreaker. I mean, you could always renovate, rip it out…"

He knew he was frowning as he pulled in a deep breath, wondering whether she was teasing. He shook his head. "I'm renovating nothing. I suppose you're right. Now I'll have to find a furniture store." He looked around and then back to her as she leaned on the light marble counter. Damn, she had a gorgeous smile. She really was beautiful, gorgeous, a breath of fresh air.

"I know a few. And look at this kitchen! You should take it for this alone. While you're cooking, you get to look at that view."

He was already sold, but seeing this place through Chris's eyes and hearing the excitement in her voice sealed the deal. "You like to cook?" he asked, curious. Jill cooked some, but Jake had done most of it, and of course he could find his way around a kitchen. Damn, he needed Jill out of his life, out of his head.

"I do."

"Really, are you any good?"

She wasn't smiling, and he wasn't sure what to make of it as she looked around and then back to him. Even with glasses, the vibrant blue of her eyes really popped. But it wasn't just the color. When she looked at him, he knew she really was looking at him and not somewhere else.

"Oh, yeah, I am. You should try my lasagna, and I make a mean pot roast, apple pie, jambalaya… It's a good thing I don't have a kitchen like that or someone to cook for, or I'd spend every waking minute in the gym, having to run it off. Because I also like to eat what I cook."

He couldn't imagine that. She had a great body, slim —perfect, really. "I'd love to try your cooking sometime, give you free access to my kitchen anytime you want. It would be a hardship, but I think I could handle it." He couldn't help teasing her as he leaned on the counter next to her.

She didn't say anything, and he wondered what she was thinking.

"Well, what do you think?" the realtor said. "Is this one a keeper, or do you want me to find some more places for you to look at?"

Chris had become so quiet. Jake made himself look over to the realtor, seeing the hopefulness. "I'll take it," he said, then dragged his gaze back to Chris. "You're right. This is perfect."

Chris didn't say anything else, just gave him a soft smile.

"Great! I've got the paperwork here," the realtor said.

Chris was still quiet as Jake slid his hand over her bare arm. There was something comforting about touching her. He hadn't expected to feel this way. "How about dinner?" he asked her. "I'll sign everything, and then we'll get out of here."

He wondered for a moment whether she'd say no. She didn't step away as he let his hand linger, his thumb brushing the soft skin of her arm. He wondered what she was thinking.

"I really shouldn't..." she said.

"Of course you should."

There it was, that smile that was just Chris, not big and flashy, just there. "Okay, dinner sounds great."

Ten

Jake didn't know what had changed, but as he pulled up in front of his hotel after signing all the paperwork, paying a deposit, and walking out into the still warm night air, he realized Chris wasn't just a distraction. He parked in front after the quiet ride back. He figured she was tired, and he was on edge, living something that didn't feel quite so wrong anymore.

Chris appeared confused, and her brows crinkled. "This is your hotel, isn't it?" She gestured to the window.

"It is," he said. "Food's great. I don't know Phoenix like you do, but I know the restaurant here, and I know it's good. It's okay, isn't it?"

She shook her head as she pushed up her glasses again. "Yeah, sure, it's fine, but it's a school night. You'll drive me home, right?"

He took in the teasing as he pulled open his door. "You know I will."

Chris was already out of the SUV when he came around. She was so attractive, athletic and slender. Being with her, talking to her, he welcomed her company. He handed the valet his keys and then set his hand on Chris's back, opening the door for her and following her inside. The air conditioning was blasting, and she shivered when he touched her.

"You cold?" he said. "I can run up to my room and grab a sweater that won't fit you."

There it was, that smile as she looked up at him and rubbed her bare arms, her heels clicking on the floor. He had to fight the urge to slide his arm around her.

"I'll be fine as long as we're not sitting under the AC vent." She tapped his chest as he walked her into the darkened dining room. In the candlelight, the maître d' was making his way over. "You don't need to run up for a sweater, but thanks for the offer."

"Mr. Wilde, nice to see you again. Two for dinner?" The maître d' was an older man with light hair in a white dress shirt and dark jacket.

"Chris is a little chilled from the AC blasting. You have someplace a little warmer?"

"We have a table by the fireplace."

Jake rested his hand on Chris's lower back, and she started walking in front of him, following the man. Her long legs were turning a few heads, and Jake let his gaze linger on an older balding man whose eyes were glued to her ass. He knew the moment the man had seen him. He didn't have to say a word. The man quickly looked away, back to the older woman he was with.

"How is this?" the maître d' asked Chris as he pulled out a chair for her at a nice corner table, out of the way at the back of the restaurant. The small gas fireplace threw off a subtle heat.

"Perfect, thank you so much," she said, taking a menu, as Jake pulled out his own chair.

"Can I get you two a drink to start?"

Chris was already looking at the menu, and she flicked her gaze over to him. "You know, I'll just have a water. Actually, hot water and lemon."

Jake pulled in his chair. "Make that two, but mine ice water."

Chris was staring at the menu, and she tapped her finger to her lip. He wasn't sure what to make of her expression. "You know, I've never eaten here, Jake, and now I know why. The orange chicken salad is almost twenty dollars. For a salad! Sure, there's some orange and chicken in there, but twenty dollars?" She leaned in toward him. She was so fucking interesting and damn smart, exuding a strength he wasn't used to.

"Well, I do get paid the big bucks," he said.

She actually rolled her eyes and gave her head a shake, then gestured to him. "So you're buying tonight? Because I'll be pretty pissed if you tell me it's my turn to buy and stick me with the bill. You may get paid the big bucks, but us cheerleaders have to work another job." She was so cute and so matter of fact.

"Would never stiff you, Chris. Not you." He let his gaze linger, taking in the shape of her face, more square than round. Her lips were full, and her chin, nose, everything seemed so perfect. The air between them had filled with a tension he couldn't remember ever having felt, not like this.

She cleared her throat. "You gonna look at your menu? Because I have to tell you I'm starving."

He smiled wide and reached for the menu, then flicked it open, sliding the wine menu off to the side.

Within a few minutes, a waiter he couldn't remember seeing before, in a white shirt and dark pants, returned with their drinks.

"You two ready to order?" he said. "Or do you need a few more minutes?"

Jake hadn't even looked at the menu. "What do you recommend tonight?" he asked.

"The prime rib is very good, sir. We actually have a special on it tonight."

"Sold," he said. "That was easy. Chris?"

She flicked her gaze over to him, then closed up her menu. "Prime rib sounds good." She gave the waiter a polite smile. Was she uncomfortable or tired?

"Great. Two prime ribs. Would you like wine with that? We have a wonderful Malbec that pairs perfectly." The waiter was young, tall, lanky.

Jake felt heat coming off the fireplace. "You want wine?" he said, looking to Chris. "I don't drink much, but we're kind of celebrating tonight."

Would she say no? The waiter was picking up the menus.

"I could drink a glass of wine," she said. "The Malbec sounds good."

"Well, I guess that settles it," Jake said. "Two glasses."

The waiter gave a nod of approval. "Great. I'll get your order in and be back with your wine."

Jake turned to Chris, who leaned back in her chair. "You warm enough?"

She smiled and let out a sigh. "Yeah, this is perfect."

No, she was perfect.

"You know, Chris, thanks again for today. You turned finding a place into something kind of fun, if that's possible. Tell me about yourself, Chris, your hopes, dreams…" He really did want to know what made her tick. She was amazing.

"Me, you want to know about me? Not much to tell."

He made a rude noise as she lifted her steaming mug and blew on it before taking a sip. "Now, I find that hard to believe. You're always sitting there, listening to me. I really want to know about you. You work for a law firm but won't let them take advantage of your time. You've got boundaries, and I really admire that. You're a cheerleader on the sidelines while all of us jocks take the limelight, and you're pretty damn easy on the eyes."

She put the mug down, unsmiling. He really didn't know how to read her, he thought, as he accidentally bumped her leg under the table.

"Sorry," he said. "I take up a lot of room."

"Yeah, just another big guy," she said. "Don't worry about it." She said nothing for a moment, and a comfortable silence descended. Then she said, "Okay, well, I enjoy being a cheerleader with the Cardinals. For me, it's about getting out there, being part of the team. And I like working for Jennifer. She gets some interesting cases. Thought about going to law school, but I'm not sure if I want to take it on right now. It would be a big expense, a lot to swing with cheerleading. I figure I'll know when the time is right." She shrugged as if she were embarrassed.

"That sounds great. If it's what you want to do, you should go for it."

The waiter arrived with two glasses and a carafe of red wine, and he poured a taster sample in Jake's glass. Jake realized what he was supposed to do, so he tasted it, not that he knew much about wine tasting. One pretty much tasted the same as another to him. "You're right. It's good," he said and nodded, and the waiter filled both their glasses.

Chris raised hers. "Here's to your new place."

He clinked his to it. "For which you now must come shopping with me to pick out all the furniture I need, since you talked me into the nice unfurnished one."

She smiled brightly. "Oh, I think you'll be glad in the end that I did."

"So you heard all about my disaster of a relationship," he said, "but you mentioned only in passing that something didn't work out for you. What happened? I mean, I just can't believe you haven't been snapped up by someone."

She took a rather large sip of wine, considering what to say. "I just haven't met the right guy, I guess. I need someone who understands me. You know the song, looking for a guy who's looking for a girl like me. There's a lot to it. I thought he was the one, but it wasn't mutual. You know when you're fooled, and I was, so I'd rather be alone than just be with someone, you know?"

Jake didn't miss the glances she was getting from two of the men at the bar. He wanted to slide around beside her and put his arm over the back of the chair to let them know she was taken, but she wasn't. She was his friend—a friend he realized he was attracted to.

Then the waiter showed up with their prime ribs, sliding a plate in front of each of them. "Can I get you anything else?"

Chris was already shaking her head. "No, this is great."

As the waiter walked away, Jake watched the

amazing girl who had found him at his worst and was sitting there with him now. He realized he didn't want to be with anyone else.

"I thought you were hungry?" She gestured with her fork to his plate.

He reached for the napkin and placed it on his lap, then picked up the steak knife and fork. "How is it?"

She took a bite of a slice of beef and nodded as she chewed. "Mmm, so good."

He shoved a bite in his mouth, realizing how comfortable he was with a woman he'd known only a short time. She was everything Jill wasn't, and as he looked over to Chris, who was digging into her potato, he realized what made her so different. She didn't need him, and never once when she was with him did she appear to be somewhere else, thinking of someone else.

No, just like now, when she was with him, she was really, one hundred percent with him.

CHAPTER
Eleven

Jake thought he could talk to Chris all night. Uncomfortable silence didn't exist with her. He leaned on the table after the waiter cleared their plates and they finished their wine.

"You sure you don't want dessert?" he said as he signed the bill to his room, knowing it would be charged to his credit card.

"Not a chance. I'm stuffed. This was really nice, Jake. I enjoyed dinner." She was reaching for her purse, but he didn't want this night to end.

"You feel like going for a walk?" he said. She lifted her brows, and he wasn't sure what she was going to say, so he continued: "Kind of not looking forward to going back to an empty hotel room with just me and four walls."

There was the hint of something, amusement, maybe, as she slid back her chair and stood up. "Sure, why not?"

He pushed himself out of his chair and directed the waiter walking their way to the bill on the table. His hand went to Chris's lower back, and he took in her heels as she started walking.

"Enjoy your night," was all the waiter said to them.

"Thank you," Chris replied.

"You okay walking a little in those?" Jake said.

She glanced up to him, so close to him as he pushed open the door, touching her again. There was just something about touching her, being with her. He couldn't remember feeling this comfortable with someone he'd known for only days.

"Even though I've been in these most of the day, I actually kicked them off under the table the few hours we sat in there," she said. "My feet are revived. If you're looking to walk miles, the answer is no, but a short stroll to work off dinner is just up my alley right now."

There it was again as they stepped out into the warm night, the perfect temperature, not the heat of the day but a pleasant warmth, as the sun had already set. He moved around Chris, keeping his pace slow as they walked down the sidewalk. The traffic was constant, and he realized he no longer missed the Seattle rain and dampness.

"A penny for your thoughts?" Chris said. She had crossed her arms, and he wondered if she was cold.

He gently bumped her with his arm and then touched her back again. "Always wondered why anyone said that. So who was the guy who broke your heart?"

She winced as she looked away. "Nobody I'm still stuck on. It took some time, but I got my head screwed on straight and am putting one foot in front of the other." She glanced up to him and shrugged. "He was a football player."

Anger rose in him out of nowhere as he thought of

the Cardinals players. "Seriously, someone on the team?"

The smile was gone as she stopped and faced him, so damn close. "Not anymore. As you know, players get traded all the time, and so was he. He's gone, and really, I guess I'm glad for that, as I think about it now, because I don't know how I would be able to go in there to practice and watch him at the games. I was warned not to get involved with a player, but I did, and I learned my lesson when he blew me off."

It was the way she said it that bothered him more than anything.

"He was a fool," he said, then reached over and tucked a dark lock of hair that had slid out of her ponytail behind her ear. She didn't pull away, and something sizzled between them. It was the way she was looking at him, nothing shy, confident, strong.

"Jake…" She touched his hand and didn't pull her gaze from his, holding his wrist.

"I want you." He just said it.

"Excuse me?" Her voice sounded breathless, and she shook her head. "No, Jake, you are still head over heels for another girl. I am not a distraction. I can't be. I won't be." She went to step back, but she stumbled, so he scooped her up, and she slid her arm around his shoulder, and he wasn't sure who was more surprised.

Then he couldn't help himself. He leaned in and kissed her.

CHAPTER
Twelve

She hadn't expected to feel this way. She slid her hand over his cheek as he held her in his arms and kissed her so softly, so gently. Then he pulled back, and she knew deep down that he wanted her. She wasn't a fool.

He put her down so gently, letting her feel him. Her hands ran down the length of his solid arms, and she knew this was a mistake as she stood in front of him, feeling his warm hands on her and knowing how amazing it would be to be with him. Did she really want this? That was the question sparking a war between her heart and her common sense—but her common sense had been drowned out by a glass of very smooth, very tasty wine.

"Jake…"

He touched her lips. "Don't say again that I don't want you, because I want you, Chris. I want to be with you tonight."

She reached up and slid her hand around his wrist, feeling his strength, his warmth. "I'm sure you do, but I also know you're mourning the loss of a relationship. Sure, I'm here now, but am I not just a distraction, a warm body that you hope will ease your hurt? Jake, I can't be that, as much as I want you…"

He lifted his hand and brushed her cheek with his thumb, looking at her in a way that said she was special. "Hey, I see you, Chris. And yeah, you're right, I'm hurt, but I'm not looking for a distraction for the night to forget her. That's not why I want you to stay." He was so damn close to her, and she knew he wanted to kiss her again. It would be so easy.

"If I stay, then what?"

He let his hand fall away and stepped back, jamming his hands in his hair. It was long, messy, and she had to fist her hands, because she would have given anything to run her fingers through it. But she could see she'd hit a nerve.

He let out a rough laugh. "Damn it, I don't know. I just want to be with you because no one has made me feel this good in a long time. I don't know what you're looking for me to say. I know you want me, but I can see you're worried about something, that I'll screw you and tell you to get lost. That's not what this is, Chris."

She could feel his passion in the way he looked at her. She pulled her arms over her chest and glanced away, nodding, before she looked back to him.

"You're cold."

She shook her head again. "We should head back. You'll give me a ride home still?"

There was no smile for her now, and as his heavy gaze settled on her, she felt his disappointment. "Of course I will. I'm not an asshole. Come on." He took a step toward her and started walking with her, and he let his hand touch hers. It was just instinctive, his touch, and she slipped her hand into his so easily, just like that, as they strode back to the hotel.

"I didn't mean to push, you know." He let out a heavy sigh, and she felt the gentle squeeze from his hand to hers, something else unexpected.

"There's just something about you, Jake Wilde, that I can't figure out. Why me?" She didn't know if he'd answer as she glanced up, seeing his confusion as they walked closer to the hotel.

He shook his head. "Not sure what you mean, Chris. Why not you? I mean, you're pretty damn special."

She didn't know what to say. As they approached the door to the hotel, Jake let go of her hand, slipping his to the small of her back as they stepped inside.

"My SUV, did you park it underground?" he said to the valet, who nodded and said something she couldn't make out in reply. "No, that's fine, I'll get it." He touched her again and told her, "I just have to get the keys at the front desk."

When she said nothing, he stopped and touched her arm, saying, "You okay?" as he slid his hand over her cheek again. Damn, why did he have to be so perfect?

"Yeah, fine, thanks, Jake."

He smiled down at her and angled his head. "Let's go."

It was so easy this time when he reached for her hand as they walked up to the front desk and the young man behind it.

"Hi, I'm Jake Wilde. I'm in room 1426. You have the keys to my SUV." He pulled out his wallet and ID, and Chris looked away, taking in the hotel, the brass, the glass, the niceness.

Jake touched her arm. "Let's go," he said again.

They strode to the elevators and pressed the down button, and the doors slid open with a ding to reveal an empty elevator. She stepped inside, and as the door slid closed, he pressed the button to the parking garage and then stood beside her. She slid her hand back in his as the elevator descended, and she looked up to him.

He must have understood what she wanted, as she could see it in his eyes when he said, "You sure?"

She forced herself to nod. "Yeah, I am."

The elevator slowed and dinged, and Jake pressed the button for the fourteenth floor. The doors slid closed again, and he stepped in front of her, right against her, sliding his hands over her cheeks and leaning down. He kissed her deeply.

"Jake…" Her heart thudded as he pulled back, pressing her arms above her head, against the glass. He kissed her hard and passionately, a deep kiss so she could taste all of him. His tongue brushed hers, and she breathed him in, his scent like a forbidden fruit her body craved. She realized she'd probably die if he pulled away, because it felt so damn good to feel his hands on her, touching her, kissing her. He was so strong and male around her.

The elevator dinged vaguely in the back of her mind, and Jake pulled away. All her emotions were jumbled, her nerves exposed and raw. She wanted Jake, the sexy football star, who was holding her hand and pulling her out of the elevator and down the hall to his door. Her legs were trembling, and each step she wobbled unsteadily on her heels when she was normally so surefooted.

He glanced down at her. He was so tall that even in

her pumps she had to look up, as his shoulders were level with her nose. When she did look up, it was into those amazing, secretive deep eyes, which she'd never seen in a man before. She wondered if he was the type of guy she'd spend a lifetime getting to know only to discover she'd just scratched the surface. He opened the door to his room, and it was dark, so he flicked the light on as she walked in.

She heard the door close behind her as she took in the king-size bed, all white with pillows and a plush, inviting duvet. Then she realized, as she stared at the bed, that this probably wasn't such a good idea.

Run. She heard the word in her head, faint and said without any conviction, but she didn't want to. She wanted Jake to touch her, to want her badly, as much as she wanted him. She was so damn confused, but then his hands were on her again, running up her arms. He was behind her, sliding his arms around her waist and pulling her against him, into him. It was quiet in the room, and she could hear his breath, her heartbeat, and nothing else.

She leaned back into him as he reached for the strap of her purse and slid it down, letting it fall to the ground. He leaned down and pressed a kiss to her neck and then her shoulder so tenderly, so gently, and then he turned her around, and she slid her arms up over his shoulders, and he pulled her right against him and kissed her deeply. She could feel every hard inch of him as he maneuvered her back until her legs touched the bed and they folded beneath her. He was over her, all that hard muscle so inviting and ready for her to touch. She wanted to touch all of it, every part of him, and it was killing her not to be able to run her hands over his nakedness. She fisted her hands before sliding them over his biceps and magnificent sculpted arms, feeling his cotton shirt between them.

"You don't want this? Or you do?" He leaned in and brushed his lips lightly on her chest, just above her breast, and she felt a spark of desire shoot through her. He kept kissing her slowly, teasing over her shoulder, her neck, then hovering just above her lips, waiting for her to say no. But her heart was hammering so hard that she was fast losing the battle to push him away. She didn't want to think anymore. She just wanted to feel, to feel Jake all over her, inside her, to just be there with him now.

"Yes, I want you."

He slipped off her glasses and reached out to set them on the nightstand. He smiled above her, his eyelids heavy as he watched her with such desire and then kissed her, angling his head, sliding his lips over hers as he deepened the kiss. He moved on top of her, all that male hardness, and she could feel his desire pressing into her. He reached for the elastic of her ponytail and yanked it out before running his hands through her long hair.

His hand slid down and over her breast, touching her through her blouse. Her nipples tightened, and she wanted to free herself from her clothing, to feel his skin next to hers. She hooked her fingers under his shirt, pulled it from the waistband of his jeans, and ran her hands up over the skin of his back, feeling the bunch and pull of his muscles.

His hand was on her leg, pushing her skirt up higher, tracing the soft skin on the inside of her thigh, and he touched her through her underwear. Oh, good Lord, she wanted him. She allowed him to settle between her legs. His hands were so big, and he pulled her underwear down and slipped a finger inside her. She tried to spread her legs, but the damn skirt was still there. She was kissing him, and he pulled away to take his shirt off, so she reached around and unfastened her skirt, squirming out of it and then quickly unbuttoning her blouse and slipping it off as he kicked off his jeans and underwear. He was naked, and damn, did he look good. She pulled her bra away, adding it to the pile of clothes on the floor.

"My God, you're beautiful," he said as he climbed back onto the bed, his knees slipping between her legs, and pulled her down onto her back, pressing her legs wide. He wasn't shy, and he was so ready for her as he kissed her, slid his hands over her breasts, the flat of her stomach, over her ass.

She ran her hands over him, between them, feeling him and his length as he pulled back and just looked at her. He opened the bedside drawer without a word and pulled out a condom. She should have been thinking, but at least he was. She watched him cover himself before he joined her on the bed again, kissing her again, touching her again, moving over her.

He pulled her closer and moved her legs around him, and then, so slowly, he slid inside her.

CHAPTER

Thirteen

Never before in his life had he felt such pleasure. He wasn't thinking about love or a commitment or tying a woman to him. He was lost in the moment of complete ecstasy, just feeling something other than his heart being shredded in a thousand pieces. Breathless, he could feel her hand tracing circles over his back, and he needed a second because he was positive he'd died and gone to heaven. He lay on top of Chris, pushing her into the mattress, her legs still wrapped around him, and he didn't want to move.

"You still alive?" she said, which had him wanting to laugh, but all he could get out was a grunt. She was so damn amazing, and her touch was absolutely wonderful. She was sweet, the most responsive woman, and he just wanted to stay forever, feeling this bliss.

"Jake, you're heavy." She patted his back. "Come on."

He pulled away and ripped off the condom, then climbed off the bed to dump it in the trash. She was lying on top of the duvet, watching him, and he was speechless at how gorgeous she looked in his bed. Her silky long hair shimmered with a hint of red, a shade he'd never seen before. He stepped closer, back onto the bed, then lay beside her, slipping his arm under her head and pulling her closer so she could snuggle against him. He kissed the top of her head and just held her. The way she tightened in his arms, he could feel that she was thinking, and sometimes thinking was the worst thing a person could do—especially in moments like this. At least there was no awkward silence. He should say something to her, something like *Stop thinking too much. Just be here with me now.*

"Jake, what is this?" She didn't look at him, but he could feel her breath whisper across his chest. She licked her lips, and he could feel himself stirring again. "Jake?" She prodded him, sliding her hand over his chest, the question hanging in the silence between them.

"I don't know. Does it have to be anything? Can't we just be here together? I want you, you want me. Can't that be enough? You are so perfect, and I just want you here with me."

She breathed out a little hard, rough. "I suppose. I just don't want to be confused that something is what it isn't. I want all the cards on the table. I need to know. I need to be clear on your expectations, because here is the after, and sometimes this is where reality hits hard."

He didn't let her go at first, tracing his fingers down her back. Then he ran his hand roughly over his face. "Reality is holding you in my arms, where you feel so damn good against me. Cards on the table? I just want to be with you. That's all."

She said nothing else, and he wasn't sure how to keep it light between them. She wasn't some stranger.

He liked her. She was amazing. He liked being with her. He'd never done the friends with benefits thing, and he wondered whether that was what she wanted. Even though he didn't know her well, he sensed that she just wasn't that way. Some women and men could pull it off, remain emotionally detached, but he couldn't, and he was pretty sure she was the same.

"Is that what you want it to be?" he asked. He had to, because for the first time in his life, he didn't have a clue how to react. If he said the wrong thing, he could hurt her, and he realized he didn't want to hurt Chris. She was important to him.

Maybe he'd said the wrong thing, as she pulled away and rolled onto her back, looking up at the ceiling. "I don't want to confuse this for something it's not, Jake. I get attached. I have feelings. I need you to be clear. Please be upfront with me right from the start. That's all I ask. Yeah, I wanted you, and I caved, and now…"

He sat up, leaning on his arm, looking down at her. He reached over and slid his hand across the flat of her stomach. "You're wishing you'd made me drive you home, that you hadn't given in. Well, you have to know I have no regrets."

She was looking right at him. "You sure? Because it wasn't that long ago you were pining for another woman." She was so damn direct, and he felt the slap.

He sat up, looking back to her. "Don't bring Jill into this."

There was a light knock on the door.

Chris lifted her head and started to sit up, glancing at it. "You expecting someone?"

"No. Didn't order anything, either."

He was about to ignore it when whoever it was

knocked again. Maybe it was the maid. Maybe they had forgotten to put towels in the room or something.

"Just a minute. I'll put the 'Do not disturb' sign out." He climbed off the bed, and so did Chris, who hurried into the bathroom and shut the door behind her. Jake reached for his jeans on the floor and slid them on before striding to the door and opening it.

He stared into amazing brown eyes. Her dark hair was now longer, pinned back at the sides, her white shirt loose under a dark green jacket over blue jeans. He couldn't for the life of him believe Jill was standing in the hallway outside his door. What the fuck kind of joke was this?

"Jake, I'm so sorry!" She hadn't waited for him to say something before she slid her arms around his waist, and for a moment, he had to remind himself to breathe. She was trembling, crying, and this was definitely one of those unbelievable moments.

He heard the bathroom door behind him, and he could feel Chris standing there, watching. He had to make himself look over to her, and what really gutted him was the horror staring back at him. She was watching Jill, who was still touching him, and he felt like a world-class asshole.

He knew he needed to say something, but when he opened his mouth, all that came out was, "Chris, this is Jill."

"I'll be out of here in just a minute," was all Chris could think to say in that dreadfully awkward moment when she stumbled out of the bathroom wearing one of the white terrycloth hotel robes, over-whelmed with the awful feeling that she'd done some-thing wrong. Her hair was a mess, and she could still feel the effects of having Jake inside her. She dragged her gaze over the bed where she'd been moments earlier. Of course, her clothes were strewn all over the floor by the bed with his. It wasn't a large room, so he couldn't hide anything.

"Chris, wait…" Jake was saying, but she couldn't look at him. She heard the door close and glanced back once to see him stepping toward her, but Jill was standing by the door, and Chris felt she was the one who wasn't supposed to be there.

She grabbed her clothes off the floor and did her best not to look at the woman who was suddenly there after kicking Jake to the curb. The awkwardness lingered as she stood up, clutching her clothes, and took in the man who had been touching her intimately moments ago. Maybe the horrible feeling of shame was because Jake had done nothing to make this better for her, just stood there out of reach with a look as if he'd done something, or maybe it was her. Guilt was guilt, and that was all she was seeing all over his face. What a fool she was.

She said nothing as she walked around him, and he didn't reach out, not once. In fact, he jammed both his hands in his hair as she raced back into the bathroom, not missing the hateful look Jill tossed her.

She closed the door and sagged against it for a second.

"Who is that?"

Why did the walls have to be so thin? She had heard the accusation, but she couldn't make out what Jake said in reply. She shut her eyes for a second. Why had Jake let Jill in? Why hadn't he shut the door in her face and told her to go away?

"Chris." There was a knock on the bathroom door.

She jumped away from it, dropping her clothes on the counter. She couldn't find her underwear, and she wasn't about to go back out there to find them, so she slipped off the robe and tossed it over the bathtub before pulling on her bra and shirt, slipping on her skirt, and pulling the door open.

Jake was still there, and so was the girl, wearing a pained look as if she were the injured party. Chris stared at the woman who had jerked Jake around, and she looked away for a moment, appearing embarrassed. Good, she should be.

Jake said nothing.

She had found herself in a triangle, but she'd be damned if she'd stay in it. Jill nodded in the awkward silence, her gaze connecting with Chris's, though there was nothing understanding or friendly there. Women could be vile, spiteful creatures when it came to their men, but this woman had pushed Jake away. Chris just hoped he would set her straight. *Please stand up for me.*

Jake was rubbing his hand across the back of his neck, and his expression had Chris searching the door and entrance for her purse. Awkward—she hated this.

"Chris," he said again, this time reaching for her arm as she grabbed her purse, which was on the floor by a pair of his shoes. The hotel room was too damn small.

"You know what?" she said. "Give me a second and then I'll be out of here." She looped the strap of her purse over her shoulder and walked over to the bed to reach for her glasses on the bedside table. She kicked her shoe out from under Jake's shirt and reached for it just as Jill bent over to retrieve her other shoe by the garbage can.

"You looking for this?" She held it out in her slender hand.

Jake actually stepped forward between them and took the shoe from Jill, and the gaze he tossed her was one Chris couldn't have made sense of, not for the life of her. Was he angry? He was something, and she needed to be far away from him.

He stepped closer and handed her the other shoe, which she slipped on. He put his hands on her shoulders as she stood right in front of him, feeling naked, wondering where her underwear were. She couldn't look at him, so she stared at his shoulders—his wide, magnificent, muscled shoulders. They were so strong, and she had to fist her hands to remind herself not to touch him, because she realized he didn't have his head screwed on straight or a handle on the fact that he was being jerked around by a woman who had just invaded their privacy, and he'd allowed it to happen.

"Don't run out," he said.

She shook her head. Was he crazy?

She looked up, because his hands were still on her, but he didn't say anything else, so she patted his hand and said, "I'm leaving, Jake." She couldn't spend one more minute there, because out of all the embarrassing things that had happened to her, this was the first time she had ever felt like the other woman. "I will never be that girl," she said in a low voice, seeing the door and wishing she were already on the other side of it.

As she stepped around Jake and he let her go, she felt daggers coming at her from a woman she didn't know, a woman who shouldn't have been there.

"Chris, seriously, wait a second," Jake said, frustration in his voice, as she was halfway to the door, her heart pounding.

"I'm going to go," she said. She had made it all the way to the door on shaky legs, feeling a slight tremble inside of her. Maybe it was shock, but as she went to pull the door open, she was hit by a wave of sadness.

"Chris, wait." He was right behind her, and he pressed his hand to the door to stop her from leaving, but she couldn't turn around, couldn't look up at him, because then he'd see the tears swimming in her eyes, threatening to spill over.

"Yes?" she said, forcing her voice to remain calm past the ache welling up in her chest, in her throat. She blew out a breath and pressed a hand to her mouth when she felt a sob bubbling up. She pushed it back and prayed he wouldn't touch her, because then she wouldn't be able to hold it together. She could feel his heat, though, how close he was. She just needed a minute to find the stairwell so she could slip away alone where no one could see her.

"Just give me a minute here and then I'll drive you home," he said. For a moment, she thought he would touch her.

"No." She cleared her throat roughly. What, did he expect her to wait in the hall, where someone could walk by and see her at her worst? "You stay here. I'm a big girl. I can find my own way home."

"Look, at least let me give you some money for a cab." He was patting his pockets, and the shock of him tossing her money made her feel cheap and whorish. Didn't he get that? She squeezed the strap of her purse and stared at the dark wood of the door, feeling an icy splash of reality that was enough to have her pulling it open and glancing back to him.

"No, Jake, I don't think so."

She stepped out of the room, hit by overwhelming relief at the sight of the elevator. Forget the stairs. No one was there, and she jammed her finger on the button. She didn't look back, because she could feel Jake watching her as she waited for the longest few seconds of her life. Then the elevator dinged, and the doors slid open. She looked back only once to see Jake standing bare chested, leaning in his open door.

"I'm sorry," he said.

But instead of saying anything, she stepped inside the elevator and jabbed the button for the lobby, then pressed the button for the doors to close. She sagged against the back of the elevator as it started to move, feeling numb, gutted, and once again like such a fool.

Jake wanted to kick himself as he watched Chris hurry into the elevator. The way she had looked back to him, he knew she wasn't okay. He was entirely responsible for the shadow of hurt he had seen in her eyes. He stepped back into the quiet room and closed the door, then pressed his hand against it, just leaning there for a second, staring at the dark wood. When he turned, Jill was standing there with her arms crossed, staring at his bed.

Everything about this was wrong. He pulled a hand over his face and took one step, then another, and all he could think was, *Why now?*

"I don't understand." It was all he could get out, gesturing toward her. Jill turned to him, staring at him now as if she were the one who had been wronged, watching him watching her. It was so much like a stand-off. She still wore her dark green jacket, her bag looped over her shoulder.

He took in everything about her, wondering when his illusion of her being the center of his world had begun. She'd meant everything to him. Everything he did and planned and decided, he'd always thought of Jill first, but in those few seconds of staring at each other, he realized something was different for him now.

"What are you doing here?"

She furrowed her brow, and he took in how different her eyes were from Chris's big, bright blue ones, which had hidden an unexpected strength and kindness. She had listened to what he had to say. She had understood everything and more.

"Remember, you called me over and over…" She gestured to him, then turned to the bed again as if she had walked in on them. Yet she was the one who had walked out on him. He just stared at her, realizing she'd never once asked him how he was or just listened to him.

"Well, that was awkward," she continued. "Walking in on you with another woman… I guess you really have moved on."

He stepped around her to pull open his drawer and yank out a t-shirt, which he pulled on over his head. He couldn't look at Jill. His cheeks heated, so he bent down and picked up his shirt and Chris's lacy white underwear with it. She'd run out without underwear under that slim-fitting skirt.

He grabbed his socks and underwear from the floor and pulled open the bottom drawer he used to stash his dirty clothes, then tossed everything in and shoved it closed. He could feel Jill watching him. Maybe she was waiting for him to respond, but what could he say? He was furious, but at whom? *Himself.*

"Why are you here?" He ran his tongue over his teeth and crossed his arms when she took a step toward him. He felt himself tense when he realized she was going to touch him.

Maybe she thought better of it, as she pulled her hand away and lowered it to her side. She didn't come any closer. "I've been thinking a lot."

He cocked his head, wondering how many weeks she had needed to think about what he was offering. Was it second thoughts she was now having? He made a rude sound. "About what?"

"You're not going to make this easy on me. I should be furious with you, walking in here and seeing you've hopped into bed with someone else."

"Seriously?" The way she stood there so close to him, he wondered if she expected him to reach out to her. "You walked out on me how long ago? I asked you to marry me, and you said you still had feelings for my brother. My brother!" He fisted his hands as he let them fall to his sides, feeling burning anger. He'd never yelled at her before.

For a moment, she seemed wary. Maybe she feared she was messing with a sleeping lion.

"I called you over and over," he said. "I waited like a fool for you to come back to me. I begged you. I would have crawled through hell for you." He pumped his fist in front of himself, then jammed his hands in his hair as he stepped away, turning to look at the closed door, through which a girl he'd never have wanted to hurt in a million years had just left. When he looked back at Jill, she was watching him with such sadness, a tear running down her face. She swiped it away, something about her that was so familiar.

"You're right. I wasn't being fair, but I was being

honest." Her voice trembled, and she hiccupped, fighting tears.

Right, how could he forget? Jill was a crier. He'd spent many a night holding her in his arms, trying to soothe her tears away. She wasn't as strong as Chris. He couldn't help comparing them and seeing all the shortcomings in Jill that he'd never really seen before. Now he realized he didn't know what he wanted. He'd fought for Jill for so long, believing she was the one, what he needed, but Logan had said long ago, at a time when he was mourning his own lost love, *We always want what we can't have.*

"You were with my brother?" he asked, though he already knew she was. She'd told him as much, but for how long? From the moment she walked away from him?

"Yes! I told you I was confused," she cried out.

"How long?" he spit out through clenched teeth. He needed her to say it, to tell the truth, all of it.

"After I left you. I called him. I've been with him since after Christmas."

"So all this time I was calling you, you've been with my brother. Did he know it was me calling, making a fool of myself? Were you two laughing at me, at what a joke I am?"

She didn't say a word. She touched her fingers to her mouth. She was shaking.

"Ah, I see. Of course you told him." He could read her so well, especially when he didn't want to.

She gazed down at the ground, embarrassed.

"So let me get this straight: You ran back to my brother after I was there for you, after what he did to you, dumping you and picking up a woman right in front of you? I gave you everything of me, offered you everything, and you ran back to him?" He actually laughed, but it sounded cruel to his own ears. "So why are you here, showing up in Phoenix at my hotel, then embarrassing my friend as I try to move on? Trying to shame me and her as if I cheated on you, when you were with my brother? You should be ashamed. What is it you want from me?" He leaned in, feeling the burning deep inside of him as he watched a woman he'd once felt so much for, so much that it had hurt to breathe when she'd walked out with a piece of him.

She took a shaky breath as she glanced away.

"For the love of God, just spit it out."

"I'm pregnant," she said, looking right up at him, her eyes now red from the tears she wiped away.

It took him a second to realize what she'd said as she stood there, breathing out.

"You have to be fucking kidding me!" He pressed his hands to his face, then let them fall away as she took a step back. Was she scared of him? All he could do was stare at Jill, who appeared uneasy and had just yanked the rug right out from under him.

"Thanks for picking me up." Chris ran her hands through her long dark hair and flicked it back, trying to tidy it. She wondered how she looked as she climbed into Myles's red Corvette. The way he let his gaze sweep over her, she could feel the bite of disapproval. He didn't have to say a word.

"You look like a fucking mess." There it was, her wonderful supportive brother making her feel worse than she already did. He pressed the gas and pulled away faster than he needed to. "So who'd you sleep with? Do I want to know?"

He changed gears and pressed the gas down so she was pinned to the seatback. Yeah, this car had power, and her brother was obviously pissed. She had no idea what he'd been doing when she called.

"I'm sorry. I didn't want to call, but I didn't have enough cash for a cab. Do you mind dropping the inquisition? I just want to go home." She could have walked to a bank machine, but she didn't know where the closest one was, and she could have been walking for a long way in the dark in shoes that were starting to hurt her feet. The way she was dressed this time of night, with her hair looking as if she'd just rolled out of bed, well…she didn't want the looks she knew she'd get.

He let out a heavy sigh. There really was something going on with him. "Sorry, but look at you. Seriously, outside a hotel? Come on, Chris, you're my sister, not some two-dollar whore, but that's what you look like right now." He changed lanes, still driving faster than he should.

"You can be damn cruel sometimes, Myles."

He glanced over to her, and there it was, a flash in his blue eyes, the fire that reminded her he wasn't the kind of guy who just listened. He could crush her, at times, with his criticism. "Cruel, really? Look at you! So who's staying here, Chris, and what the fuck are you doing popping into some guy's hotel and letting him screw you? Everyone in that hotel would know by taking one look at you what you've been doing, like some second-class call girl. You're dressed the part, too."

He was right, but did he have to be so crude? "Yeah, well, it wasn't planned—and could you just drive me home without the lecture? I'm not a child."

"Maybe not, Chris, but you're acting like one," he snapped. There was nothing remotely understanding in his voice.

Seriously? She was about to tell him to stop and pull over. She'd find another way to get home. "You know, Myles, could you maybe, just once, be my brother and stop being an asshole? What is going on with you? Because I know you well enough to know you become nasty when your back is against the wall, and you're not above taking whatever you're dealing with out on me."

He glanced her way and then back at the road. She didn't miss the hesitation, the tell he had when something was weighing on him.

"We've always talked to each other, but you haven't been yourself for a while, not since you fumbled during the big game," she said. "Then there's been the slew of injuries, one after the other, your shoulder, your knee. Are you drinking, too?"

He made a rude sound under his breath, and she thought he cursed as he shook his head and gave the car gas to blow through the yellow light just as it turned red. "Should be asking you the same thing, Chris. What's going on with you? You still haven't answered me on who you were with. Do I know him? Who's staying at that hotel?"

"Why, so you can go back and pay him a visit?"

The last thing she wanted was Myles knowing any more of her shame.

"Damn straight. Any guy who has you walking out of his hotel room to find your own way home is a guy who needs to be taught a lesson," he snapped. "Who was it, Chris? Some guy you picked up, someone I know? You getting yourself in a mess again?"

There it was, the reminder of Troy. She wondered if he'd ever let it go. "I'm not some slut, Myles. I don't pick guys up. And this isn't Troy. The misunderstanding—"

He slammed on the breaks when the light in front of them turned red, and the seatbelt dug into her shoulder. "Troy was not a misunderstanding, Chris. You got a call from the cops because you wouldn't leave him be. Stalking is serious."

"I wasn't stalking him. I was just…"

The light turned green, and Myles gave the Corvette

gas and geared up. "No. I got a call from Troy to talk you down because he had called the cops on you, and he was damn serious about the stalking charges. Look, Troy was a first-class prick, and that was his way of telling you to get lost. I don't want you getting caught up in something like that again." His voice softened, and she wondered if he'd spare reading her the riot act again. That call from the cops was one she'd never forget, and she still wondered if all the guys on the team knew or just some of them.

"It's not the same thing this time, and it doesn't really matter. We're friends. I shouldn't have to explain it to you. I was with a friend, we had dinner, and it just kind of happened, so can you drop it, please?"

He gestured to her with one hand before putting it back on the gear shift. "Do I know him?"

"It was Jake Wilde."

"The guy who's here to replace me?" He glanced over to her, and she could see the question, the horror in his eyes.

"I'm sorry. I like him. He's a really great guy."

"Oh, Chris. Haven't you learned anything after Troy? I told you to stay away from the players on the team. I don't want to see you gutted like you were. Most of these guys aren't looking for commitment with a nice girl like you. They want no strings, a quick fuck, and so long, baby, get out of my bed and my life and don't call me."

For a second, she wondered if he was talking about himself. He wasn't seeing anyone, but she knew he wasn't a monk, into some things she was pretty sure she didn't want to know about. She'd heard the talk from some of the girls who'd been with her brother. It was a picture she didn't want in her head. She made herself look out the window.

"You don't get it, Chris. He's not going to call. He's done with you. So you need to be okay with that and leave it be. What happened with Troy…I don't want to ever see you suffer like you did. He played you. He had fun. When a guy leaves…"

"I know! You've told me a hundred times." She cut him off before he could finish. "It was his way of saying get lost, so long, because I wasn't important enough for him to give me a second thought."

"Yeah, that's right, and the way you pushed it—"

"I know, okay?" She gritted her teeth, spitting the words out. She didn't want to hear any more lectures about a time in her life she wished she could forget about forever. "I thought there was more. I fell in love with him. I was an idiot. I thought if I kept calling, he'd realize that he cared for me. I was hurting, and I needed to hear from him that it was over, but he never gave me that courtesy. Maybe I'm not as 'take it or leave it' or 'love them and leave them' as you and Troy, but what he did to me, calling the cops, saying I was harassing him…that wasn't fair. I didn't harass him. I was devastated that he left, that he wouldn't call me back. He never said one word about ending anything. He just left when he got his offer. That was cruel and unjustified."

"Maybe so, Chris, but he was also a coward, and calling the cops on you was his way of having them tell you what he didn't have the balls to tell you himself. It was a crappy thing to do, I agree, but you've got to be smarter about guys like that. If a guy is really into you, he's going to call you. He's going to pursue you, so don't be giving it away for free. You need to make him earn it."

Her brother had a way of talking that felt at times more like a slap-down. He pulled up in front of her three-story walkup, and she touched the handle, about to open the door and climb out, but instead she slid around on the dark leather and faced him.

"Thanks, Myles, really."

He nodded, staring straight ahead, then turned to her as she listened to the purr of his engine idling. "Sorry for hassling you." He glanced away again. "Look, I've made some decisions as of late. I'm considering retiring."

Of all the things she'd thought he would say, that wasn't one. "What? Why? Is this because of what happened?" He would know what she meant: the fumble that had cost the team their spot in the playoffs. She knew some things just weren't forgivable.

"Partly. I have a lot to consider. I'm making just under a hundred thousand a week, and I've saved nothing. This is make or break time, Chris. Reality is that I'm likely to be dropped, and everything out there, including the endorsement deals, is drying up. No one's knocking on the door of the guy who was responsible for fumbling in the playoffs. I don't have a big college degree like some of these guys, so I've started diversifying lately, invested in a franchise. But I've got an offer on the table to coach."

She'd never in a million years thought he'd consider coaching. "Where?"

He dragged his gaze over to her again. "University, Vanderbilt. They came to me a while ago. They've been holding the position, but they need an answer."

"Are you going to take it?"

He watched her for the longest time, then took a breath and tapped the wheel with his hand. "Yeah. You have to know when to stop holding on to something that's over. And this team here, playing, I can't lie to myself anymore. It's over."

She'd never heard her brother sound so sure of himself. "I think you're doing the right thing."

His mouth twisted with an odd smile as he looked over to her again, the brother she loved, who wasn't cutting her down or criticizing her. "I think you should come with me."

She hadn't expected that. "I can't just pack up and leave. You're talking Nashville. I have a life here…"

"What kind of life do you have here? A job with a law firm you tolerate, a sideline job as a cheerleader? These are not solid career choices. Come on, Chris. I want you to think about it. You need a fresh start, to get away from these players, all of them."

She never wanted to sit by the sidelines, but as she thought of Jake, she said, "Can I think about it?"

"Yeah, think about it. We'll talk tomorrow. But I'm serious, Chris. Sometimes you've got to know when you're done and it's time to move on. I can see you heading again to a broken heart, I don't want that for you."

She nodded, more to herself than to him, because on some level she knew he was right. She slid open the door and climbed out onto the sidewalk, then closed the door and held up her keys from her purse so her brother could see them. She knew he was waiting for her to open the door. He could be an asshole at times, but she knew he had her back when it counted.

She shoved the key in the lock and stepped in, and as soon as she did, she heard her brother drive away. Her eyes ached, her head was weary, and as she started up the stairs to her suite, she realized she wanted nothing more than to curl up on her bed and have a good cry.

Having Jill stay in his hotel room wasn't what he'd expected. He figured he was still reeling from the little bomb she'd dropped on him. The ache in his chest was still there the next morning as he realized what he'd done—no, what he'd set in motion, believing at the time that it was what he wanted.

He heard the shower running as he sat on the edge of the bed, his bare feet on the dated carpet and his cell phone on the bedside table, and all he could think was that the woman he really cared for had run out of his room the night before because of Jill, because of something he'd done.

"Well, you really screwed things this time," he said to himself as he picked up his cell phone and saw no messages.

He needed a minute, and he needed to talk to Chris, to see if she was okay. Hell, he wasn't okay after last night. He thumbed through his phone and spotted her name, hovering over it for a second before calling her. He pressed it to his ear as he stood up, listening to one ring and then another as he walked over to the window. The curtains were wide open.

"Hello, this is Chris. I can't take your call. Leave a message and I'll call you as soon as I can."

He lifted his head at the voicemail. "Chris, it's Jake. I wanted to call and check on you this morning after last night…" He paused. "Call me, please. I want to talk to you, see if you're okay." Damn, he didn't know what else to say, so he ended the call.

"You never told me what that girl means to you."

He hadn't heard Jill come out of the bathroom. He pulled his hand over his stiff neck and squeezed it as he took in her standing there with a towel around her wet hair and the robe he thought Chris had worn the night before. The awkwardness lingered as he tossed his cell phone on the dresser by the TV he'd watched once.

"How'd you sleep?" He had no intention of talking about Chris with her. It just didn't feel right.

"So the girl I caught you with is off limits? I see." She licked her lips as the distance in the room grew. "I slept fine, considering." She gestured between them. "You didn't have to sleep on the pullout. It couldn't have been that comfortable. I could have taken it."

"It's fine. I'm going to grab a shower."

He stepped around Jill, and she reached out and touched his arm. At one time, her touch had meant everything. But all he could do was stare down at a woman who had run right back to his brother. Yet now here she was. He didn't know what the fuck he was going to do.

"I realize I pushed you away, and what I did wasn't fair to you, but I was scared," she said. "I'm still scared. That's why I had to come and see you."

Maybe it was the way he stared at her hand that had her lifting it from his arm. Jake walked around her and pulled open the top drawer to fetch a clean t-shirt, jeans, socks, and underwear, then closed it, holding the clothes.

"Well, I guess it's a fine mess, then, Jill." If he was being honest, it was a mess he'd created. His conscience prodded at him, but he pushed the thought away. He could be an ass when things didn't go his way, as he could tell by the hurt that shadowed her expression. "Look, we'll figure it out, okay?"

She lifted her head, and a soft smile touched her lips. Maybe that was why it was so instinctive to lift his hand and touch her cheek, as he'd done many times before. She leaned into his touch, but for him this was far different from every other time. It didn't feel right, so he pulled away and stepped back.

"Jake, for what it's worth, I'm sorry for the way I treated you. I can't help the way I feel. I'm so torn up over all of this."

"You're still in love with my brother? Yet you're here."

Did he really want to know? He waited as she glanced away, hesitating, indecisive. She appeared so torn. He'd seen that expression many times before. Maybe he just hadn't been willing to find out what it meant. He'd been scared to know.

"There's a lot to discuss, Jake. I'm confused. All I know is I'm pregnant, and it's changed everything. I didn't plan it, but I wondered if you did. I was so mad at you. You'd never been careless before. But the way you kept pushing… At first it felt wonderful to be wanted, but when I realized how deep I was in, and you wanted it all with me, I panicked, because it had suddenly become more than what it had started out as."

By the way her expression changed, he knew she was holding something back. Then she shook her head as if pushing whatever it was away. A woman with secrets. Jill, he realized, had many. Part of her had always seemed to be out of reach, a part she hid from him.

"Maybe you're right," he said. "Maybe I was careless, so head over heels for you that I never stopped for one minute to realize you were just stringing me along. Was Samuel always in your mind when we were together?"

She wouldn't look at him. Damn, he'd never expected this. No, she was right. Why hadn't he figured that out before?

Her cell phone started ringing, the sound muffled, before she could say anything to him. She strode over to her navy purse, which was sitting on the dresser behind him, and glanced hesitantly at him before reaching in and answering it. At any other time, he'd have stayed and listened, then asked her who it was. But he'd lost interest. He was so tired of her secrets and holding back, so he walked into the bathroom and closed the door.

He took his time standing under the hot spray before his stomach rumbled. He needed coffee and food, so he turned off the shower. Then he heard a knock at the hotel room door. Maybe she'd ordered room service, which was what he should have done.

He dried off and pulled on his clothes, then tossed the towel over the hook on the back of the door, the fan stirring the steam from the shower in the background as he pulled it open.

"You order something to eat?" he started, then froze,

his chest tightening as his gaze landed on his brother. The way Samuel was watching him, he knew there was no love lost. There was Jill, dressed in the day before's clothes, her wet hair slicked back.

His brother gestured to the beds. "So who slept where?"

He only shook his head as he walked over to the dresser, reached for his wallet, and shoved it in his back pocket. His brother was sporting a new look, with messy short hair, and his expression said just how pissed off he was.

"Great, this is just great," Jake muttered as he walked past the two of them. "I took the pullout. You happy?" At this point, he just wanted some coffee. He sat on the bed, reached for his sneakers, and pulled them on.

The energy in the room was stifling. No one said anything.

"So you ran down here to my brother?" Samuel snapped. He paced and then leaned against the wall. This hotel room wasn't big enough for the three of them, and Jake wasn't interested in being part of this triangle anymore.

"Look, Samuel, things have become complicated." Jill had such a soft voice.

"I'll say," Jake said. "Look, you two want to talk or have it out or whatever it is you want to do, you go for it." He reached for his keys on the nightstand and tucked them into his back pocket. "I'm going to go for coffee, grab a bite to eat." Then he paused. He had to ask, had to know. "So is this who phoned, Jill? My brother? And you invited him up." He shook his head, realizing he wasn't expecting her to answer.

At one time, he and Samuel had been so close. Never in a million years could he have imagined the chill between them now. It was sad to know their relationship and the closeness they'd had was gone, likely forever.

"Yeah, I called her," Samuel said. "Why did you up and run, Jill? I came home from work and you were gone, and then I found your note. We've talked about this already. We decided it was better not to say anything."

"No, you talked. I listened. This isn't right, Samuel. This could be your brother's baby."

What the fuck? The way she said it had Jake turning ever so slowly to stare at her and then his brother. "What the hell is going on? Could be my baby—are you kidding me? What kind of fucked-up games are you playing, Jill?" he snapped, then glanced his brother's way.

Samuel was shaking his head. He could be so pigheaded sometimes, but this was the first time Jake had ever felt as if his brother were trying to screw him over. It stung more than anything, his brother and a girl he had been so head over heels for.

Jill was looking down at her fingers, a slight blush on her cheeks. She didn't answer him, and Samuel was staring at her hard as if waiting her out and expecting her to say what needed to be said.

"Somebody better say something."

Samuel pushed away from the wall and fisted his hands. Was he looking to take a swing at him? It was amazing: Jill didn't even look up as her hand shot out to Samuel's chest, holding him back. She must have been used to dealing with his fiery personality. She just stood there, holding her ground between them.

"I'm waiting," Jake said, "and I'm not liking what you two are up to. Stop messing with me and tell me already. What the fuck is going on here?"

Jill was still touching Samuel, all three of them at a standstill in his hotel room. Not a scenario he wanted. It hurt that he finally understood he'd always come second to his brother with Jill. Whatever was going on, they'd discussed and planned it together, and Jake was the odd man out.

"Jill, are you going to tell him, or should I?" Samuel was going all alpha on her, and she started to say something to him, giving him all her attention. No one needed to fill in any more blanks or explain to him that he didn't stand a chance here. But then, he realized, this was a fight that had long since lost any appeal for him.

"Tell me what? Someone better fill me in."

"Samuel, I can't. It's not right." Jill was talking as if he wasn't even in the same room, and the cryptic shit was really pissing him off.

"We're getting married," Samuel said to him, dragging his gaze over to him, nothing friendly in the way his brother was watching him.

"Stop it, Samuel!" Jill cried. "Don't be so cruel. Jake, I was kidding myself. I was angry and hurt over what Samuel did, but I never stopped loving him. I realized, when you asked me to marry you, that I couldn't love you like that. You were my friend, a very, very good friend who was there for me. I love you like a friend, my best friend. When I found out I was pregnant, I hoped it wasn't yours."

"It may still not be," Samuel said. "You don't know

for sure. We won't know until the baby's born." He touched her hand.

Watching the two of them felt so much like having a knife turned in his back. Cruel, hurtful. Damn, he needed to get out of there, because this nightmare was only getting worse. He didn't know where it had come from, but he let out a rough laugh that didn't make him feel any better in this messed-up situation.

"So let me get this straight," he said. "Jill, you left me and went back to my brother, and you hopped right into bed with him? Talk about blurred lines, baby. You knew before that you could have been pregnant with my kid, so I'm confused about why you're here. I thought you came here to do the right thing—or is it that you're trying to figure out which brother to marry now?"

"No! I came here to tell you I was pregnant, but I know you already knew, because you asked me on the phone. You have no idea how many times the question crossed my mind when I found out. Did you plan this? And yes, I slept with your brother, and maybe it was wrong of me to do what I did, but I can't help the way I feel. I love Samuel. I always will. I don't love you, Jake, not like Samuel."

He knew that of all the stupid, clingy things he'd done, not using protection was something he'd thought he'd never stoop to. He wished now he could go back and undo all of it.

"You went after my girl, Jake," Samuel snapped.

"No! The moment you moved in on another woman in front of her, you lost her, but then, Jill, you seem to have forgotten all of that. Maybe you two do deserve each other."

Samuel could move fast when he wanted to, and he

had Jake pushed back over the dresser. A clock fell to the floor, a tray of glasses crashing to the carpet with it. Jake was caught off guard, but he jammed his hands between them and punched Samuel in the stomach, then elbowed him in the face to get him to back off. Blood dripped from his nose, and Jill yelled, moving between them. He took in his brother and the anger that would likely always be there.

"I'm done with this shit," he said. "I'm going for coffee, something to eat, and when I get back, Samuel, I want you gone."

As he pulled open the door, he didn't look back at his brother and the woman he'd been so twisted up over. He walked out into the hall, toward the stairs, and let out a heavy sigh in the empty stairwell as he started down. The one person he'd wanted so badly, Jill, was exactly who he didn't want now.

CHAPTER
Eighteen

When Jake let himself back into his hotel room, carrying a takeout coffee, he expected it to be empty. Instead, he found Jill sitting on the bed with a tearstained face. When she glanced up at him, she looked so miserable.

"I'm so sorry, Jake," she whispered, and she really sounded as if she was.

He squeezed the paper cup of lukewarm coffee, looking around to make sure his brother wasn't still there. "Where's Samuel?"

"He left. I told him I needed to talk to you, which was why I came last night."

He nodded and sat in the chair against the wall. Jill clasped her hands and shoved them between her legs. She looked so nervous, something he'd never seen in her before, not with him.

"Are you staying with my brother?" he asked. Maybe he needed all the ugly truth.

"Yes, I am. I know without a doubt that I love Samuel in a way I can't love you. I need to be with him.

I wish I could love you, because you're better for me." She appeared so sad.

Jake nodded. At one time, this would have gutted him. Now he just felt numb. "Well, you're not better for me," he said, and she flinched. He hadn't meant to sound like such an asshole. "So what are your plans?"

"That all depends on you."

He downed the rest of the coffee and then shrugged. "I don't see how any of this depends on me." He gestured to her, because he couldn't figure out what she really wanted. He realized, too, that he never had understood Jill or what she was thinking.

She sighed. It sounded so soft, as if she'd put a lot of thought into whatever it was she needed to say. "You are an amazing man, Jake Wilde, and you are the best friend a girl could ever have. I never really thought of the consequences of what I was doing with you. It really sank in when Samuel came after me. Seeing him here this morning…you and Samuel, as close as you once were, will end up hating each other. I don't want that. I need you to forgive me, to forgive him. I'm responsible for this, and I don't want to carry that. I never should have gone to you when Samuel hurt me."

Was she serious? "Jill, it doesn't work that way. I can't just forgive and forget. Having a do-over is wishful thinking. It's something you and I don't get to do."

She didn't nod or pull those deep brown eyes from him. "Do it for me. Please, Jake, I don't think I can live with the fact that I'm the reason you and Samuel hate each other. You two were best friends, and I learned early on when I was with Samuel that it meant you were always there too, his little brother. But seriously, Jake, if you're honest with yourself, you aren't entirely blameless here. You were his brother, and even though what he did was really bad, you moved in on me, his ex. I was vulnerable, Jake. You knew that."

He hated having anyone point out his screwups and toss them back in his face. But he knew she was right. After all, Logan had warned him he was treading on dangerous ground. "You were willing, Jill, so it's not all on me."

She lifted both hands in surrender. "No, it's not. I hold a lot of blame. I was hurt and not thinking clearly, and you provided me a strong shoulder to lean on. What happened was inevitable, I think. You're charming, you're unbelievably handsome, you're a great listener, and you made me feel better."

"But you never loved me." Even as he said it, it stung, but not as it once had. He knew he deserved better.

"No. I wanted to, tried to convince myself that I did, but you can't make yourself love someone."

"And the baby?" He had to know what was going through her head. "You left me and went right back to my brother and climbed into his bed, and now you have no idea if it's his or mine. Did you do that deliberately?" He'd never have thought she'd be capable of something like that, knowing she might be pregnant with his kid and sleeping with someone else so she'd never really know.

"Did you plan to get me pregnant?"

He didn't want to answer. He knew what he'd done.

She let out a heavy sigh. "You don't want to answer, but it's written all over your face. I can be honest about this much. Yes, Jake, I went back to Samuel and slept with him so I wouldn't know for sure."

"So you really don't know whose baby this is?"

A tear slid down her face, and she shook her head. "No. It just happened."

"If this is mine, I won't simply walk away, you know. This child will have a father, and it won't be Samuel. It will be me."

She fisted the duvet and didn't look away. "He feels the same. The thing is, though, Jake, I love him, and I want to have a future with Samuel. I need you to be okay with this, to be okay with me and Samuel. I need you to let Samuel raise this baby, to let it go if it's yours, to be okay with it being his."

He leaned forward. "What is this, Jill? You showed up here last night, barged in on me and my friend, and practically chased her out of here, shaming her, making me feel as if I cheated on you. Were you expecting me to wait on the sidelines, alone?"

She stood up from the bed, her cheeks flushed. "I'm sorry. That wasn't fair of me, but I didn't expect you to be here with another woman, and I was jealous for a moment. I didn't have a right to be, I know that. All I can say is I'm sorry."

He nodded but couldn't look at her. "I see," he said. And he did see.

She reached for her bag, on the floor at her feet, and slipped it over her shoulder, then for her green jacket on the bed behind her.

"So where is Samuel?"

"He's waiting for me downstairs."

"And what happens now?" He watched as she fiddled with her strap, nervous.

"I am going back to Seattle with him. I'm going to marry him. I need this to work, Jake. I need you to let us be so we can move on. When the baby's born, I'll let you know whose it is."

He shrugged again. "So that's it. I have no say, and we let the chips fall where they may?"

She sighed and looked over to him. "I'm sorry, Jake. I never meant to hurt you, but this is the way it needs to be."

If it had been any other time, he'd have stood up, gone to her, and said anything to change her mind. He'd have gone after her, fought for her. But that time had long since passed. He stared at a woman who'd had him so twisted up he couldn't even see how wrong she was for him. Then she walked to the door, pulled it open, and didn't look back.

As he stared at the closed door and crumpled the empty paper cup, he wondered why the choices he'd made had turned out so badly.

CHAPTER
Nineteen

Chris taped up the last of the boxes in her living room and took in the small one-bedroom apartment she'd lived in since moving to Phoenix. The sun was shining in through the open sliding glass door, and she could hear the traffic on the street below. For a moment, she wondered if she was making the right decision.

She tapped the box and took a minute to look around her place, which was packed up and being emptied. An incredible sadness squeezed in her chest even though she knew her brother was right: It was time to leave Phoenix for a new start. She reached for the black Sharpie and pulled off the top, then scribbled *Living Room* on the last box just as she heard a knock at the door.

"You forget your key?" she called out as she climbed over a box. Myles had said he would be right back, but when Chris pulled open the door, her heart sank. Jake stood there, wearing blue jeans and a fitted green t-shirt. She sucked in a breath. Damn, he looked so good.

For a moment, they just stared at each other.

"Can I come in?" he finally said as the awkwardness lingered.

She should've said no, closed the door in his face, but the way he watched her, staring her down, she just couldn't. She was a sucker for this man. Her downfall. Her brother was right. She had no sense when it came to footballs stars. She squeezed the doorknob, willing this not to be happening again.

"Why not?" She stepped back and kicked a box aside as he strode in, looking around.

"Are you going somewhere?"

Chris closed the door and took a second to figure out what to say. "I'm moving to Nashville. Myles accepted a coaching job and talked me into going with him. A fresh start somewhere no one remembers all my screwups. He was right about one thing: Phoenix hasn't been good for me."

He dragged his gaze over all the boxes, and she didn't know what to make of his confused expression as he let his blue eyes settle on her again. "Why, Chris? Why are you leaving?"

She couldn't believe he was asking her that. "You're kidding, right? I would think, Jake, that you'd be happy. You won't have to avoid me at the games, at practice. Just think of it as me making this easy for you." Maybe it was the way he was staring at her as if she'd lost her mind that had her lifting her hands, gesturing helplessly, before letting them fall to her sides again. "Jake, I've just made one too many mistakes…"

"Like me, am I a mistake?" He stepped closer to her but didn't touch her, and she didn't know what to make of the hurt staring back at her. How could he be hurt?

"Let's see. Ten days ago, there was a knock on your hotel room door, and who was there but Jill, the girl you were pining away over, after you'd just finished screwing me. That was my wakeup call, Jake. You have your girlfriend back, and I'm not interested in being someone's seconds. I like myself. I'm a good person, and I have feelings. I hurt, I bleed. Let's just chalk it up to a fun night we had and leave it at that. I knew better than to climb in bed with you, and yet I did it, so shame on me."

He breathed out roughly, giving his head a shake. "Don't do that," he said. "And, for the record, I don't have Jill back." He leaned against her bookshelf, so close to her that she could've reached out and touched him. The way he said it, she wondered if he was mourning the loss.

"So is that why you're here, because it didn't work out?" She pulled her arms over her chest, furious because he was still spinning it. "I'm a great listener, Jake, but not in this. I do not want to hear about the girl who showed up at your door when you were with me. I don't want to see her in your arms…"

"She's pregnant," he bit out, cutting her off. "But she thinks it may be my brother's. She doesn't know."

Was that why he was here now? She angled her head. "Well, that is quite a mess, isn't it?" She took in his unease, the way he shook his head. The last thing she wanted to be was a sounding board for his broken heart.

"My brother showed up, too. Apparently, she plans to marry him." He took a step, fidgeting, and pulled his hand over the back of his neck again. She could feel his tension.

"You know, Jake, how fucked up that sounds, a

woman playing two brothers? But do you have any idea how I felt, walking out of that bathroom and seeing her there? You let her in, and I was the one in a robe, picking up my clothes while feeling the daggers she stared me down with, making me feel as if I were the other woman…" She shook her head, angry again. "And now you're here to use me as a sounding board because that woman has you wrapped around her finger and you can't even see it. From where I stood, she looked like your girlfriend. But some girls only want a guy so another girl can't have him."

He was suddenly quiet. It felt so good to finally use her words.

"Look, Jake, I like you, but you need to figure out what you want. She dropped a bomb on you, but have you asked yourself, her, or your brother where this leaves you?"

"Where does this leave me?" The way he said it, he sounded confused by her question. "Hell, I don't know, but I know I don't want any of that situation. I'm so sorry for how I made you feel."

The way he was watching her, Chris wanted to step back and move farther away, because Jake had a way about him that wasn't good for her. "I'll never play seconds to anyone, Jake, and I'm not an afterthought."

"Of course you're not. Chris, you're wonderful, you're my friend, and I never realized how much I've come to care for you in such a short time. When I opened the door and Jill was there, I realized how wrong I'd been about her, and how I couldn't even see what she was doing. You were right about so many things. Jill and I could never work, and I couldn't see that until you came into my life. When you left and I watched you get into the elevator alone, I wanted to kick myself. She's not you."

What was he doing?

"And the baby? What are you going to do when the baby comes? You have an incredible mess, Jake."

"I don't know. I haven't figured it all out yet, but if it's my kid, I want a relationship with it. I will be involved. What kind of man would I be if I just walked away? I wouldn't do that. I know it's a mess, and I'm not making excuses for what I've done, but there'd be no me and Jill even if she wanted to come back to me. When you have your eyes opened, they're opened for good. I know my brother and Jill want me to just go away, to stay out of the baby's life."

It made her uneasy, the way he was looking at her. She had to look away.

"That's good, Jake. It's good you can see it, but it doesn't sound like a great situation. I'm sorry for that." She made herself look at him. Damn, he was so handsome, and the way he was watching her, the tension that oozed, she knew he could feel it.

"There you go again, being you," he said.

She made herself pull in a breath, and maybe he realized how uncomfortable she was, as his gaze seemed to soften. "Did you know that I was involved with Troy Sutherland?" she said. Why was she telling him this? She'd never told anyone. It was too painful to share how pathetic she'd become.

He frowned, thinking. "Didn't he play right wing with the Cardinals before he was traded?"

"That's him. Myles warned me off, told me to stay away from the guys on the team. He said to me over and over they weren't for a girl like me. I didn't listen. And I really loved the way Troy seemed to be interested in me. I thought it was real." She knew she had all his attention, and maybe he had some idea where she was going. "I was into him. I fell head over heels, but apparently he wasn't as into me. I was something to pass his time, some amusement. So when he was traded, he just up and left. I was devastated, even tried to tell myself that he cared, that he just didn't realize how much.

"So I called a lot, left messages, because when you're with someone, sleeping with her, you don't just up and leave, right?"

Jake was suddenly so still, not pulling his gaze from her. She knew she had all his attention.

"When he didn't call back, I made excuses, you know, that his phone was off, or he was busy, anything. I lost count of how many times I called. Sure, he finally called me back a few times, kept it light—friend stuff, kind of like what you're doing now. Told me to be good and take care, no offers to come on out and visit or move in with him, no telling me he missed me. The distance was in his voice, but I wasn't ready to hear it."

She gestured between her and Jake. "I was hurting, I ached, because it wasn't casual for me. I was head over heels, blindly in love, so I pushed harder. He called my brother, told him to talk to me, to get me off his back, to basically fuck off and go away, to stop calling. But I didn't listen, because I was so in love with him and so desperate. I told myself Myles didn't really understand. So when I picked up the phone and made that last call to Troy, he had the cops knocking on my door the same day, and they explained to me that he didn't want to be contacted anymore and I needed to stop calling him. If I didn't, I could find myself in serious trouble." Her chest tightened as she relived that humiliating moment. For the first time ever, she'd felt as if she were a criminal. "So hear me, Jake. I care deeply, I get hooked, and I won't go there again with a football player. What happened between us, Jake, was a mistake—a mistake I'm not willing to repeat."

She made herself walk into the kitchen, standing on the other side of the half counter. At least it was a half wall between them. She took in the way his brow knit, how quiet he was. Maybe he had realized what a nutjob she was.

"I'm sorry, Chris. What Troy did…that's a shitty thing to have happen to you. I probably understand better than anyone what can push you to do something that stupid. But this isn't the same. I'm not Troy. I would never do that, not to you. Damn, Chris, I guess I really am making a mess of this, because I really fucked things over with Jill and with you. I wanted her so badly that I couldn't see it wasn't her I wanted. I was looking for a forever thing. I guess, being such a dumbass, I thought it was with her. Until I met you. Chris, please don't go. Don't move. Stay, stay here with me. Give us a chance. Maybe I'm not saying this right, but for days I've kicked myself over what happened…"

"Jake, I don't want this. I can't let myself get pulled into you. You're a catch, and I can see myself falling hard for you, but you're still so wrapped up in Jill that I'll be the one left on the side of the road with a broken heart. She'll show up again and again for different reasons, a fight with your brother, or she changed her mind, just like she did at your hotel room, and you'll go running to her and open your arms and let her walk right back in. You didn't fight for me there. You let me be humiliated. You let her stay. You chose her!" She hadn't meant to yell, and she willed herself to pull it together. She took a breath and blinked.

"Chris, Jill and I are done," Jake said. "There's no coming back from that. I don't want her. When she showed up at that door, I felt as if someone had sucker-punched me. I couldn't pull my head out of my ass. It happened so fast. If I could go back, I'd do it differently, handle it better. It's you I want. It's you, Chris. I want to be with you. Please just give us a chance. Give me a chance to fix it. I'm not perfect, and I screw up a lot, but, Chris, I'm the most loyal motherfucker there is. I won't ever toss you to the curb, not you. And maybe I should say this, but I'm glad Troy did what he did, because you're not with him."

She glanced down to her hand resting on the counter, to her short nails, and then walked as calmly as she could to the door. She squeezed the knob again, willing her hand to stop shaking. She made herself pull open the door. "I can't take the chance, Jake. I won't let you hurt me. Take care of yourself. I really mean it."

She wondered for a moment whether he was going to argue with her, as he just stood there, angling his head as if trying to think of something to say to convince her. He took one step and then another but stopped in the doorway, and he lifted his hand, letting his fingers touch her cheek, letting his thumb skim over her bottom lip. It took everything inside her not to lean into his hand, to reach out and touch him.

"I'm sorry," he said, "so sorry for all the hurt, but I'm not Troy. Please, Chris, think about it. Don't go. Stay. Take a chance with me, because I really, really believe that you and I could do amazing things together, and I can feel myself falling for you and building something truly amazing. I was a fool with Jill, but I mean it when I say I didn't know what love could be until I met you." Then he pulled his hand away, breaking the touch that had felt so good, and ran it over her shoulder before he leaned in and pressed a kiss to her forehead. Then he left.

She listened to the creak of the stairs of her walk-up as Jake left, and her heart thudded. Her hand trembled as she closed the door and set the deadbolt before leaning against it. Why was he doing this? Why did he have to be so damn cruel and say what he had said? She couldn't do this again. She couldn't be that girl and take the leap of faith he wanted her to take. No, she couldn't do it. He didn't mean what he said. He couldn't mean it.

All she knew, as she touched her forehead where he'd kissed her, was that everything about Jake Wilde and what he'd said scared the hell out of her.

CHAPTER

Twenty

How could he have let her go? He hadn't had a choice. He'd begged, laid his heart out, and yet here he was, alone, as he lifted his hand to the bartender and gestured for another beer. He took in the glass behind the bar and the empty stools beside him as he remembered the hurt on Chris's face. She'd always been there for him, and he'd never understood how deep her fear of being hurt went.

"Charge to your room?" the bartender said as he slid another pale ale in front of him.

"Yup, keep them coming." Jake lifted the bottle and took a swallow, glancing at some suits at a table nearby and a few women at another. The sun was bright through the windows as he took in the traffic out front, the people on the sidewalks of a city he barely knew.

As he heard the ring of his cell phone, he pulled it from his back pocket and took in the familiar name on the screen. "Was I supposed to call you back?" he said upon answering.

"You were." Logan always got right to the point. He

was the one constant in Jake's life, a brother who loved him and understood him better than anyone else had. He lifted his beer and took another swallow, then let out a sigh.

"I suppose you heard," he said. He'd be surprised if Logan hadn't.

"I spoke with Samuel. He called to tell me he was getting married. I didn't know what to say, especially when he told me who he's marrying." Logan sounded so tired on the other end. Running interference for his brothers required something not many people had. He waited for the "I told you so."

"She's pregnant, too," Jake said. He didn't miss the way the bartender looked over to him, having heard, of course. Jake slid around on the stool.

There was silence on the other end, but it was the kind of silence that came from shock. He wondered whether Logan was trying to figure out what to say.

"She doesn't know whose it is. Could be mine, could be Samuel's." Might as well get it all out so Logan could lay into him again, but there was still silence, then a squeak in the background—maybe the chair Logan was sitting in. "You're awfully quiet for someone who always has a lot to say about my business, especially when you think I've messed something up."

"How are you doing?" Logan asked. That wasn't what Jake had expected. He sounded worried, concerned.

"I'm okay, considering. I don't know, Logan. You warned me. Sometimes I just go ahead and do things without thinking of the consequences, isn't that what you pointed out to me? I wish I could go back and undo a lot, take the blinders off then and see what I can see now." A woman with long blond hair took a seat on a stool two down from him. She tossed him an easy flirty smile as the bartender walked over to her. He made himself look away.

"Sounds like you've cleared your head. So what brought on this change of heart?"

He was leaning on the bar, picking at the edge of the label on the bottle. "I met someone."

There was another rustle and squeak in the background. Maybe he'd shocked Logan again.

"You know when you want something so bad that you're not seeing the whole picture, instead seeing it for what you want it to be?" Jake said. "Well, I didn't really see Jill. I stuck her on this pedestal, and I think I made myself believe she was something she wasn't. I worshipped her for so long while she was with Samuel. I loved her. But I think maybe that was all an illusion, loving someone who wasn't really who I thought she was."

"Hmm," was all Logan said on the other end.

Jake took a swallow of his beer.

"You know, I worried about what was happening between you and Samuel with Jill. I was never okay with how quickly she went to you, and now she's gone from you right back to Samuel. It was like a yoyo—and now she's pregnant. That I didn't know. I'm sorry, Jake."

"So Samuel didn't tell you everything." He wondered for a moment what his brother had said, but why did it matter? Because they'd always been so close until Jill.

"I think he wanted my approval," Logan said. "I love you both, and I don't know how any of this can be resolved between you. If this baby is yours, what are your plans, Jake? I mean, this is a shitshow, but it's still a baby."

He wondered if this was why Chris wouldn't give an inch. "If it's my kid, I'll be its father. No one is pushing me out and denying me that right, not Jill and certainly not Samuel. I really hope you're not expecting me to just walk away and make this easier for them."

"Nope. I wouldn't expect that of you. I'm just worried about how this is all going to play out, and I'm not liking what I'm thinking or what I'm hearing from you. What about this other woman you care about? How does she fit into this picture?"

He let the phone slide away from his mouth. The blond woman was smiling at him in the bar mirror, so he lifted his beer and took another long swallow. "I don't know. I want more with her, but I think I may have messed it up and lost my chance. She's the real deal, too."

Logan was quiet again, which was unlike him. "So you're giving up? That doesn't sound like you. Jake, you've always had this fight in you, and you also wear your heart on your sleeve, which can be your undoing. When you want something, you go after it."

"This is different, Logan. She doesn't think I stood up for her. She thinks she'll always come second to Jill." And he didn't think he'd ever forget the moment she'd opened the bathroom door and seen the way Jill had thrown her arms around him.

"Will she? She sounds like a smart girl."

She was, damn smart, and when Jill showed up, he should've made his stand. He hadn't realized then how disillusioned he'd been. And now all he could see was the most beautiful woman walking away.

"No, she's not a girl who could ever come second. She's fucking amazing, Logan. Chris, her name is Chris. You'd like her."

There was another squeak in the background, then voices. "Listen, I have to go. I've got a situation I have to handle. But if this girl means as much to you as you say, and I can hear in your voice that she does, make her believe it. Convince her. If anyone can do it, I know you can. Speak from the heart." Then his brother hung up.

Jake pocketed his phone.

"Hey there, my name's Sandy," said the slim, attractive blonde. "Would you like to buy a girl a drink?" She had an amazing smile that did nothing for him.

Jake slipped off the stool and stood up, shoving his wallet in his back jeans pocket. "No thanks, Sandy," he replied, then started out of the bar to the lobby.

As he took in the bank of elevators, he thought of Chris. He'd poured his heart out, but he realized as he jabbed the button to the elevator that words wouldn't convince her. He stared at his image in the large mirror between the elevators, just another good-looking football player. With Chris, words were meaningless. It was what he did that mattered. She needed to see it. Damn, how many times had Logan said it, that actions speak louder than words? If he wanted Chris, he had to show her he would fight for her.

Twenty~One

He loved the feel of the football in his hands as he stood on the field in the late morning sun. "Wide receivers specialize in pass-catching. Our job is to run passes and get ourselves open and in position for the pass. Sometimes we need to be the block. Some people don't think of wide receivers as being tough, but remember, kids, to play the position of wide receiver, we have to be tough." He pointed to his head, taking in the eager eyes of the twenty kids watching him. How old were they, nine, ten? They were so young and impressionable, the second-grade class he was mentoring in gym, and he'd never felt so damn nervous.

"And it's that toughness you need to have when you catch that ball across the middle." He snapped his fingers and pointed out to the middle of the field, gripping the football. "You've got to go fast, quick, knowing you're going to take a hit from a linebacker who's got maybe thirty or forty pounds on you. These guys are aiming to take you out. It's what they do."

Some of the kids' eyes widened.

"But you're faster, quicker! Change directions so they can't get you. You need to be sharp out there and know everything going on all around you and who's where. Just remember that the game for a wide receiver is just you and the quarterback. You need to be on the same page, thinking the same thing. It's like a moving chess game, and when the attack comes to take you out—"

"Okay, we don't attack here, though, kids," interrupted the plump middle-aged teacher wearing what looked like a fishing hat.

This was public relations, Jake reminded himself again. He needed to do this to polish his image, as his coach and sports agent had said, and what better place than with a group of kids in the public school system? He took in the teacher. The moment she'd arranged the kids to sit in their rows, he'd understood she wasn't happy about being outside on the field.

"We respect each other out there, no 'taking out,'" she continued in a sharp tone as she looked directly at Jake. "And no tackling, because someone might get hurt." She gestured to the kids before giving him a look much like his mother would. How, again, had he been talked into this?

The kids were watching him with startled, fascinated wide eyes, glued to what he had been saying. A hand rose from a little girl in the back.

Good, question time.

"Yes?" he said as he pointed to her.

"Suzie, stand up when you talk." The teacher clapped her hands together as she stood to the side in sneakers and what he thought were yoga pants.

Jake reminded himself to breathe as the little girl stood up, with pigtails and a pink shirt.

"Mr. Wilde, when are girls going to be allowed to play football?" she said.

"Girls can't play football! That's only for boys," called out a little boy who had been sitting beside her on the ground.

"Of course we can! Girls are smarter than boys. My mom even said so," Suzie said. "She said girls can do anything; we just have to put our mind to it, is all."

"Don't be stupid," another boy said, with red hair and freckles. "A girl can't go on a field with a bunch of men. She'd get hurt. It's a man's sport. My dad said women have no business trying to play pro sports that are only for men, and football is a man's game."

"Okay, no arguing!" the teacher said. "Brent, Suzie, Mike, just so you know, women are already playing football, not in the NFL but in their own league. There are women's teams."

Okay, he hadn't expected that from the teacher.

"Well, that's stupid," the little boy said.

"No, it's not, is it, Mr. Wilde?" Suzie said, crossing her arms, waiting for Jake to back her up.

What the hell was he supposed to say? He stared at the kids, who were waiting for him to tell them…what, exactly? Because Jake was of the mind that there were some sports a woman shouldn't play. He was about to say something but stopped when he took in the raised eyebrows of the teacher. He couldn't figure out how to defuse this.

"So what do you think, Jake? Do women belong in football?"

He'd have known her voice anywhere. He turned

around and took in Chris walking toward him, wearing shorts and a white tank top, her long hair hanging straight. She was gorgeous and determined, and all he could feel was the thud of his heart.

He wondered what expression was on his face when Chris stopped in front of him. The kids behind him were whispering, and he glanced back, never before having felt this damn rattled, and said, "Hey, kids, give me a second." He turned back to Chris as he tucked the football to his side, wanting to reach out to her.

"I don't think you answered the kids," Chris said, angling her head, looking up to him. It felt so good, having her there. He could feel the smile pulling at the edges of his lips, seeing the strength in the woman who had slipped in and found a way to his heart.

"Well," he said, "I think women have the right to choose what they want to do as long as it doesn't put them in a position where they'll get hurt."

Chris nodded and made a face of amusement, he thought. "But sometimes it's the man who does the hurting," she said quietly. "You can't always protect a woman, no matter how much you want to." She was so close to him that he could've reached out to touch her. He wanted to.

"You're right, but that doesn't mean we can't do everything we can to keep you safe. It's kind of our role to look after you, to protect you, to love you."

She pulled in her lower lip and then looked away for a minute as if considering what to do next, what to say.

"Sometimes all a woman has to do is take a chance," he said. "Forgiveness is everything. A second chance, Chris, is all I ask, just a second chance to show you that it'll never happen again. You could never be second, not for me. You'll always come first." He held out his hand to her, and she looked at it, wanting to take it.

"I got your flowers," she said.

He cocked his head as she glanced away, then looked back at him. What was she thinking?

"And your key," she added in the next breath, and he felt something deepen in his chest. Hope? Maybe.

"You liked them?" he said.

She nodded. "Very much. I read your letter. You really know how to reach a girl, don't you? Did you mean it?"

He didn't know what to say to her as he thought of the letter he'd handwritten. "Yeah, I did. I want you to move in with me. I want to put you first. I want you, Chris. I mean what I say. That's your key, you and me."

She didn't look away. "What if I'm scared? I need a guarantee this will work, Jake."

He glanced past her, then settled his hand over her shoulder and let it run down her arm. "Then I'm telling you not to be scared, because I'm all in. Let me show you how much you mean to me. I want to be with you, only you, Chris. Damn, you're the most amazing woman. You turned my world upside down. I've heard stories where people say when they met the one, they just knew. Chris, you are the one. They were right: You just know." He held his hand out to her again, waiting, hoping. "I'll buy out the flower shop and send you flowers every day if I have to."

Her big, bold blue eyes softened, and she slowly smiled as she slipped her hand in his and stepped closer. "And the baby? I'm afraid you'll change your mind. I don't want to be the girl waiting on the sidelines when you're running back to her."

"There is no Jill and me. The baby, though, if it's mine, I'll be its father, but it will always be you and me. There's no Jill in the equation." *And no Samuel,* he thought, but it hurt too much to say that. "You and me together can be part of its life. I'd never walk away from that."

She stared at him for a moment, and he didn't know what she was thinking. This was make or break. Then she slid her hand in his, and he squeezed it, pulling her closer to him as she breathed out, "No, you couldn't, Jake. Maybe that's why I love you. You couldn't just walk away from a baby, a kid."

"Are we going to play ball now, Mr. Wilde?" one of the kids called out.

Jake dropped the football at his feet, wrapped both arms around Chris, and kissed her, then took in the kids watching and smiling. Without letting Chris go, he picked up the football and tossed it to the boy in the back, but the little girl beside him snatched it up and started running.

"Yup, let's go!" he called out before leaning in and kissing Chris again.

She looked up at him, her head resting against his shoulder. "So, Jake, you didn't answer that little girl's question. Do girls belong in football?"

He could feel the teasing, but at the same time, she really wanted an answer. "If I give you an honest answer, does that mean I'll be sleeping alone tonight?" he teased, pulling her closer to him again.

She rolled her eyes and slid her arm around his waist to pat his butt. "No, as long as you're honest."

He rested his chin on top of her head, loving the feel of her in his arms. "Then no, they don't belong in football—only because I don't want anything to ever hurt you or put you in harm's way."

She said nothing as she pulled back and looked up to him. She didn't step out of his arms and he could see she was considering something. Then she patted his chest, and said, "Smooth, Jake. Really smooth."

He settled both hands on her face, tucked back her long hair, and kissed her again.

Turn the page for a sneak peek of
UNFORGIVEN the next book in *THE WILDE BROTHERS*
Available in print, eBook & Audio

Junior lawyer, Samuel Wilde has an unbreakable bond with his brothers—that is, until one woman comes between them, threatening to divide the Wilde family forever.

Samuel Wilde has always been close with his brothers until one night in a dumbass move he pushed the girl he loved away, right into the arms of his brother.

Only, Jill couldn't love his kind and considerate brother, even though he was the better choice. Even after Samuel had hurt her in the most cruel way a man can hurt a woman. But one rainy night when Jill knocked on his door, he knew the mistake he'd made at the same time he didn't want his brother to have her. Only Jill soon discovered she was pregnant, the problem, she doesn't know which brother is the father.

And as Jill and Samuel's relationship turns bitter, big brother Logan steps in to not only save the brothers relationship, but may be the only one who can reason with stubborn and difficult Samuel, before sides are chosen, and the family is divided forever.

Unforgiven

CHAPTER 1

There were days Samuel Wilde didn't know what drove him. The rain soaked him, and his lungs were burning as he struggled for a simple breath, running faster and faster.

Why did he push himself to the edge, his body, his mind, as if this were the only way he could find peace, quieting the voices in his head just a bit? He knew he was an asshole. Maybe that was why he needed to punish himself. He pushed himself hard, driving himself to a place that welcomed the burn in his legs, the bite in his chest, the pace he set for himself—brutal, to the point that anyone watching might wonder what was wrong with him and why he was pushing so damn hard. He was only a junior lawyer at Pike and MacGregor, and there were days it seemed the lines between right and wrong tended to blur and morph. But his confliction wasn't just about the law. It was about who he was and about his brothers, whom he didn't know when he'd pushed away.

As he rounded a corner through the park, hearing

the traffic that had picked up, he pushed harder, faster, past the thumping of his heart, his feet pounding the pavement, and not even the puddles soaking his track pants could slow him down. He welcomed the cold rain, wishing the chill would relieve the ache that had become part of him. As he spotted the familiar corner, the coffee shop where he stopped every morning on his way to work and the high rise where he lived with Jill, there it was, that giant ache that came with just thinking of her and his brother Jake.

He fisted his hands, feeling himself being swallowed once again in the hurt and anger, just as a horn blared when he stepped off the curb. He jumped back, lifting his arm to shield his face from the splash of the car speeding curbside.

"Asshole!" he shouted, then gestured with his middle finger to the prick in the car. But the rain had picked up, and the sounds of the morning traffic drowned him out. What the hell was wrong with him, running out into traffic without looking? It seemed everything he did was wrong. His legs were shaking as he stood there, his knit hat soaked to his head. He started moving again, jogging in place, because standing still was when his thoughts became his worst enemy.

The crossing light flashed, and the early morning traffic stopped, and he forced himself to look right and then left, hearing the honks, the noise of Seattle, which at one time he had thrived in. He stared up at the gray concrete high rises, the glass-fronted businesses, and the endless steel, the endless dismal rain, which matched his mood. Another step closer to the high rise where his condo was, where Jill would be waiting, but he needed this time to himself. Just him and his thoughts, his dark thoughts.

As he reached the open glass front door to his building, his sneakers squeaked on the dark tiled floor, and he swiped his hand across his face, wiping away the water, before he pressed the button for the elevator. In the shiny steel doors, he glimpsed the reflection of his light beard, his wet gray tracksuit and knit hat, everything drenched. Droplets ran down his face, and he was unsure whether it was sweat or water from the image staring back at him. Even Samuel had to admit he looked like a thug, unapproachable, dangerous.

The elevator dinged, and he shivered as he stepped inside and jabbed the button for floor twenty-five, which was also his age. Nothing in his life was as he'd once imagined. He leaned against the back of the elevator, feeling his legs start to tighten, his heartbeat slowing. He pulled in a deep breath, knowing he still needed to stretch, as he'd pushed himself hard that morning, much as he had every day for weeks. Lately, he had embraced the burn in his body as he pushed himself to the brink, the only thing in his life he could control. It was madness, because this physical ache was something he could fix, but it did little to help the hurt and the distance he felt from his family.

The elevator slowed and opened to his floor. He nodded to his waiting neighbor, a portly man with thin hair in his sixties, who was wearing the same blue trench coat he wore every day. What was his name? It would come to him, he was sure. All Samuel knew was that he was a banker and had visitors every Wednesday night, always a different college girl dressed in some slinky number, most likely from a local escort service. He dragged his gaze away because everything about the man left him unsettled. He was really good at reading people, and knowing any more about the man was not something he wanted.

Samuel slipped his key into the lock and opened the door, then tossed his keys on the counter of the narrow kitchen, with its ticking clock and low humming of appliances.

"You're back? I didn't know you'd gone out." Jill was holding a mug of coffee as she walked into the small walkthrough kitchen. She was so quiet. She'd cut her dark hair shorter, framing her round face. She was lovely, pretty, but something about her dark eyes haunted him. He wanted her so badly despite his need to punish himself because of the growing rift dividing him from his brothers—or maybe because no one in his family had shown up the day he was to marry Jill.

"Should you be drinking coffee?" he said.

There was no smile for him as she put the mug on the counter. He pulled his wet hat from his head and peeled off his hoody, then dumped both over the back of a kitchen chair. The four-piece dinette was crammed against the wall, but then, this one-bedroom apartment was only five hundred square feet. He should really think of getting something bigger. Jill had already asked twice, but he hadn't answered. He knew she wouldn't push. She never did, never had.

"It's only one cup." She was behind him because, once again, he had walked away.

He should turn around and look at her, talk to her. He reached for the mail on the table, flipped through the bills, and then dumped them back down. "I'm going to grab a shower," he said—a hot one he could lose himself in.

"Do you want company?" she said.

This time, he had to make himself turn around, his hand gripping the door frame as he looked at Jill, at her rounded belly, at the baby she carried, and thought only that she'd been with his brother.

"Not this morning," he said. "I need to hurry. I have to meet a client."

She stood across the room. The tension between them was so thick he could feel it like a wall, so heavy that it kept him where he was, away from her. Why didn't that make him sad?

"What time are you going to be home?" she said. She crossed her arms over her breasts, which were larger now. At one time, he hadn't been able to get enough of her, touching her, making love to her, being inside her. But something had faded. He didn't know what exactly, only that it was something between them or in him that had died.

"Late," he said. "Don't wait up." He turned away, walked into the bathroom, and shut the door. He should have asked her to join him. He loved her, right? But he didn't know whether it was himself he hated or Jill, all because he, and not Jake, had had Jill first.

"Lorhainne Eckhart is one of my go to authors when I want a guaranteed good book. So many twists and turns, but also so much love and such a strong sense of family."

(LORA W., REVIEWER)

New York Times & USA Today bestseller Lorhainne Eckhart is best known for writing Raw Relatable Real Romance where "Morals and family are running themes." As one fan calls her, she is the "Queen of the family saga." (aherman) writing "the ups and downs of what goes on within a family but also with some suspense, angst and of course a bit of romance thrown in for good measure." Follow Lorhainne on Bookbub to receive alerts on New Releases and Sales and join her mailing list at LorhainneEckhart.com for her Monday Blog, all book news, giveaways and FREE reads. With over 120 books, audiobooks, and multiple series published and available at all, retailers now translated into six languages. She is a multiple recipient of the Readers' Favorite Award for Suspense and Romance, and lives in the Pacific Northwest on an island, is the mother of three, her oldest has autism and she is an advocate for never giving up on your dreams.

"Lorhainne Eckhart has this uncanny way of just hitting the spot every time with her books."

(CAROLINE L., REVIEWER)

The O'Connells: *The O'Connells of Livingston, Montana are not your typical family. A riveting collection of stories surrounding the ups and downs of what goes on within a family but also with some suspense, angst and of course a bit of romance thrown in for good measure. "I thought I loved the Friessens, but I absolutely adore the O'Connell's. Each and every book has different genres of stories, but the one thing in common is how she is able to wrap it around the family, which is the heart of each story." (C. Logue)*

The Friessens: *An emotional big family*

romance series, the Friessen family siblings find their relationships tested, lay their hearts on the line, and discover lasting love! "Lorhainne Eckhart is one of my go to authors when I want a guaranteed good book. So many twists and turns, but also so much love and such a strong sense of family." (Lora W., Reviewer)

The Parker Sisters: *The Parker Sisters are a close-knit family, and like any other family they have their ups and downs. Eckhart has crafted another intense family drama… "The character development is outstanding, and the emotional investment is high…" (Aherman, Reviewer)*

The McCabe Brothers: *Join the five McCabe siblings on their journeys to the dark and dangerous side of love! An intense, exhilarating collection of romantic thrillers you won't want to miss. — "Eckhart has a new series that is definitely worth the read. The queen of the family saga started this series with a spin-off of her wildly successful Friessen series." From a Readers' Favorite award—winning author and "queen of the family saga" (Aherman)*

Lorhainne loves to hear from her readers! You can connect with me at:
www.LorhainneEckhart.com
lorhainneeckhart.le@gmail.com

facebook.com/AuthorLorhainneEckhart

twitter.com/LEckhart

instagram.com/lorhainneeckhart

bookbub.com/profile/lorhainne-eckhart

pinterest.com/lorhainneeckhart

In the Family
In the Silence
In the Charm
Unexpected Consequences
It Was Always You
The First Time I Saw You
Welcome to My Arms
Welcome to Boston
I'll Always Love You
Ground Rules
A Reason to Breathe
You Are My Everything
Anything For You
The Homecoming
Stay Away From My Daughter
The Bad Boy
A Place of Our Own
The Visitor
All About Devon
Long Past Dawn
How to Heal a Heart
Keep Me In Your Heart

The O'Connells
The Neighbor
The Third Call
The Secret Husband
The Quiet Day
The Commitment
The Missing Father
The Hometown Hero
Justice
The Family Secret

The Fallen O'Connell
The Return of the O'Connells
And The She Was Gone
The Stalker
The O'Connell Family Christmas
The Girl Next Door
Broken Promises
The Gatekeeper
The Hunted

The McCabe Brothers
Don't Stop Me (Vic)
Don't Catch Me (Chase)
Don't Run From Me (Aaron)
Don't Hide From Me (Luc)
Don't Leave Me (Claudia)
Out of Time

A Billy Jo McCabe Mystery
Nothing As it Seems
Hiding in Plain Sight
The Cold Case
The Trap
Above the Law
The Stranger at the Door
The Children
The Last Stand
The Charity

The Wilde Brothers
The One (Joe and Margaret)
The Honeymoon, A Wilde Brothers Short
Friendly Fire (Logan and Julia)

Not Quite Married, A Wilde Brothers Short
A Matter of Trust (Ben and Carrie)
The Reckoning, A Wilde Brothers Christmas
Traded (Jake)
Unforgiven (Samuel)
The Holiday Bride

Married in Montana
His Promise
Love's Promise
A Promise of Forever

The Parker Sisters
Thrill of the Chase
The Dating Game
Play Hard to Get
What We Can't Have
Go Your Own Way
A June Wedding

Kate & Walker
One Night
Edge of Night
Last Night

Walk the Right Road Series
The Choice
Lost and Found
Merkaba
Bounty
Blown Away: The Final Chapter
He Came Back